the **americas**

Breathing, In Dust

Tim Z. Hernandez

Texas Tech University Press

This book is typeset in Monotype Fairfield. The paper used in this book meets the
minimum requirements of ANSI/NISO Z39.48-1992 (R1997). ∞

Library of Congress Cataloging-in-Publication Data
Hernandez, Tim Z.
     Breathing, in dust / Tim Z. Hernandez.
         p. cm.
     Summary: "Stories of the drug abuse, poverty, and desperation of a farming
community located in California's agriculturally wealthy heartland, home to a large
immigrant population and a high rate of violent crime. Chronicling one young boy's
coming-of-age, the stories reveal a deeper layer of sediment in a fertile American
landscape"—Provided by publisher.
     ISBN 978-0-89672-672-7 (hardcover: alk. paper)
     1. Agriculture—Social aspects—California—Fiction. 2. Immigrants—California—
Fiction. I. Title.
     PS3608.E768B74 2010
     813'.6—dc22   2009050558

Printed in the United States of America
09 10 11 12 13 14 15 16 17 / 9 8 7 6 5 4 3 2 1

Texas Tech University Press | Box 41037 | Lubbock, Texas 79409-1037 USA
800.832.4042 | ttup@ttu.edu | www.ttup.ttu.edu
www.ttupress.org

Rumi Mia
Salvador Ösel
Quetzani Lu
Destina Unica
Dezyráe Amor
For each of you, this poem

Contents

CONTENTS

*A speck of dust contains everything
in the universe.*

THICH NHAT HANH

What It Means to Say Catela

To say Catela is to say Chihuahua and Ararat and Grecia and Madina all in a single breath. To live it is a whole other tangle of vines. Forged at the bottom of a once lake, ripe with tule foliage and cattails, no eagle perched atop nopal leaf, no shining constellations or symbols of destiny manifest, nothing but darkened flesh and muscle and spade and oxen black as pitch, and a few seeds spilled from a rucksack brimming with disease and curse and karma long past due. With hunger in their bellies and prosperity somewhere on the back burner, they raked and culled and sowed and reaped day after day, year after year, on an endless workload that always concluded in death—or as they often referred to it, that hard-earned moment of rest.

And then the Southern Pacific rail was strewn across the face of it. An iron mass hurtling from one generation into the next, amidst orange groves and almond trees, cutting through the central valley like a scythe over golden necks of wheat stalk, arms and ears of corn falling in the growl of interlinked cargo flats toting San Francisco raw steel and Pacific Northwest lumber, past Devil's Ridge right up to the lip of the Pacific Ocean. Sometimes

fast enough to cloud Catela in dust, and other times, slow enough
for a child picker to peek out from atop his ladder and pelt the
iron snake with a storm of bad peaches.

And then a trading outpost, a depot, an aluminum water
tower, packing sheds, a dairy, and the pressing expansion of a new
century.

In summer, a sixty-eight-day stretch of triple digits melts the
air into wet ghosts that wriggle up from hardpan and pavement
and disappear on the horizon. Cattle ranchers hose down live-
stock, and the over-drift of manure stench lingers and gets into
everything, clothes, hair, beneath the fingernails. A group of
teenage boys drown their heads beneath an irrigation pipe, and
drink from the bowls of baseball caps. Everyone else is in shaded
quarters shelving dry ice atop swamp coolers, dunked in buckets
half-filled with water, breathing its cool mist against glowing red
skin.

December in Catela is a cloak of gray unfurling beneath mud
flaps of off-road pickup trucks hauling grove heaters to ward off
threatening frost in citrus orchards. Tendrils of smoke curl above
stacks of uprooted plum, lit in the pre-dawn before cocks crow
and eggs get fetched and fat school bus drivers warm up sleepy
engines.

Enter April, basking in her newborns, her cherry blossoms,
pink and lavender flecks on the limbs of gnarled trees. And then
Zeta daring beehives on his sister's bicycle, kicking them over and
flailing arms into the dirt when a dozen latch on and sting him
into a crying mess. The rest of the high schoolers get drunk and
pile into monstrous trucks and joyride in dry riverbeds before they
are filled with runoff from the Sierra Nevada mountain range that

rims the eastern edge. Jesus's mother places hot towels boiled in herbs over the festering welts on his back, where a farmer blasted rounds of rock salt from a shotgun for snapping off an eggplant from his property.

Everything here is built close to the ground. The highest structure is the bell tower of Holy Family Church where every day at noon twelve chimes ring over Catela, summoning the packers and pickers to lunch, while the homeless sit and watch the whole rhythm go down. A gaggle of lowly dogs bite one another on the ass and yelp and sniff around trash bins behind the carniceria, where Pato the owner tosses a boxful of bones and raw shavings and watches them fight over which one gets the gristle.

On the other side of town, Hmong women crouch in their gardens, flooding baby bok choy until the water slithers down and across the road. Meanwhile their sons and daughters mix it up with the Chicano hip-hoppers who buy, sell, and trade car parts and rims that spin at a standstill. Somewhere, the pudgy stay-at-home moms are gossiping about Jesus's sister, Ana, who lost her virginity at age thirteen in a grape field by the boys on her block, whispering about how they laid her out on raisin paper and took turns—why, she's got three kids now and no man wants her.

Beyond this, land, land, and more land, cultivated or just waiting to be. A pig farm on the outskirts. A driveway made of mud and loose gravel. A house with a dim porch light, where a young boy thumbs over a three-dimensional globe. His soft fingers roll over the mountains of Appalachia, then south to Machu Picchu. He spins the ball on its axis and lands on Sweden. Hits the lights. Puts himself to bed. And listens for the distant clacking of the passing train singing, *Catela, Catela, Catela, Catela.*

One

Animal

1983

*Concerning young Tlaloc and the tradition
of bloodletting*

Between the wire mesh Tlaloc saw the pig. It was a mass of
spastic flesh hunkered on its hams. All four legs were grotesquely
thick, like fire hydrants. Up close, he noticed its red eyeball, slimy
and pulsing in the socket. He stuck his finger through the cage to
touch the coarse yellow hairs on its snout.

"I wouldn't do that," a voice grumbled behind him. Tlaloc
stepped back.

"Look," Animal said, jabbing the middle finger of his left hand
out and wiggling the nub. Tlaloc's eyes widened. He looked over
at the cage. The pig was slumped on its side tonguing strands of
snot.

"Might look cool," said Animal, "but that son of a bitch will eat
anything you put in front of him. Even its own children."

Tlaloc stood still, waiting to see if Animal was messing with
him.

"I've seen 'em do it, mothafuckers. If they drop down to a certain weight and ain't no food in sight, they're some cannibist . . . canbalsti . . . shit, they eat each other, alright." He cracked his knuckles into his fists.

Alejandro walked out of the house, slamming the screen door behind him. "Have you seen my machete?"

Tlaloc shook his head.

"Dammit, I can't find it anywhere. Berni better not have tossed it."

"Got anything else we can use?" asked Animal.

Alejandro pulled an ice pick from his back pocket, "Only this."

"That's a piece of work, ese," Animal said, reaching for it. He took the ice pick and examined it closely, pressing the needle-point against his palm. A bubble of blood surfaced.

"Tlaloc, we're gonna need your help getting this pig into the garage, alright?"

Tlaloc nodded.

"Okay, then. Animal, when I say *now*, you pull the cage. And Tlaloc, you gonna poke the pig with the broomstick. I'll push from behind."

Tlaloc grabbed the broom and got into position.

"How should I poke him?"

"Just poke him hard, that's all."

Tlaloc and Animal nodded. When Alejandro gave the signal Tlaloc rammed the broomstick through the wire mesh into the pig's swollen back. It lurched and stood up.

"Again, do it again," his uncle shouted.

Again Tlaloc poked the pig and the cage lunged. The pig grunted and plopped onto its ribs. "Stick him! Stick him!" Tlaloc jabbed the broomstick into the pig's neck but it didn't budge. "Harder!" He hurled it into the pig's eye and the pig squealed and leapt up. He dropped the broom and stepped back.

"Pull it out," his uncle yelled at him. Tlaloc kicked the stick, and the pig rattled the cage with its jowls.

"You pissed him off," Animal said. "Look at that shit." Blood pussed from the pig's eye and dripped onto the concrete.

When they got the pig into the garage, Tlaloc's uncle called for a water break. He wiped the flood of sweat from the back of his neck with a paño, and then tucked it into his pocket and went around the side of the house to where the hose was.

"Take it easy," Animal said. "We still got a shitload of work ahead of us." Alejandro grumbled and waved him off.

Animal was a disturbing lump of a man, thought Tlaloc. His hands were knotted like tree limbs and tattooed with jagged crosses that looked like spilled ink. Between his shoulder blades, at the stem of his neck, was a round hump of muscle. The rest of his flesh was scarred and dirtied like a gas station rest room.

In his peripheral vision he saw Animal making his way to the cage. He bent down, eye level, pressed his face against the wire mesh and began making kissy noises, and whispering to it. Tlaloc was curious so he inched closer. He could faintly make out some of Animal's words.

"Mmm . . . you gonna taste good, baby, head to tail, that's right, and if I'm still hungry, I'm gonna put your huevos on the grill and barbecue me some campo sushi. Te gusta?" His gruff voice pimpled Tlaloc's skin.

"Alright, let's do this," Alejandro said. "Shut the garage door," he ordered Tlaloc.

Tlaloc made his way past the pig and tugged on the rope, and the garage door came slamming down. Except for what little light made its way through the cracks, the place was dark. The pig rustled in its cage and snorted. Animal found the light switch and flicked it on. "Where's that ice pick?" he asked.

Alejandro pulled it off a shelf and passed it to him. Animal gripped it tightly. All four knuckles whitened like knots of hominy. His eyes grew fierce. Both brows aimed downward, pointing directly at the pig.

"Mijo, when I say now, I want you to poke it again, okay?" his uncle ordered. Tlaloc grabbed the stick hesitantly and made his way to the back of the cage.

"I'm gonna unlatch the door, and you ram it with the broom. When it comes out, Animal, you grab him." Animal gritted his teeth. The veins on his forehead flicked like a den of snakes. He nodded. Even though he was now an expert at it, the thought of another round of pig-poking made Tlaloc queasy. He shut his eyes tight and before he could ready himself Alejandro was opening the cage door.

"Now!" he shouted.

Tlaloc reacted with a quick stiff jab that sent the pig staggering out into Animal's path. Animal leapt onto its back and straddled it like a rodeo cowboy. Tlaloc dropped the broom and jumped back. His uncle shoved the cage into a corner and shouted at Animal to get the hell off. But Animal laughed and responded by punching the pig on the nose.

"What the hell you doing?" shouted Alejandro.

Animal ignored him and focused on getting a firm grip of the pig's back. He grasped at the ear and yanked out a handful of wiry hairs. The pig belched and jerked. Tlaloc clinched his teeth. Animal grabbed at a roll of fat on the pig's head and before Alejandro could utter another word, he began stabbing the pig wherever his clenched fist landed. The skull. The eye. The shoulder.

The pig wailed, then bulked up and flung Animal to the concrete. The ice pick went sailing across the garage. The animal snarled its yellow teeth, bulged its eyes out, and went charging toward Tlaloc, but before it could get there his uncle cracked the broom over its wide skull. Tlaloc stood frozen. Alejandro grabbed the ice pick and flew at the pig. He slashed into the animal's flesh. When the beast dropped onto its belly he stomped it with the heel of his boot. Tlaloc heard the skull bone crack. The sound resonated off the garage walls and bounced through his stomach. His insides convulsed and retracted. Animal was back on his feet again. "Die, motherfucker!" he yelled while punching the pig in the ribs. His uncle kicked the pig in the jaw and a loud snap rang through its body. Blood frothed out in bubbles and the pig dropped down on its front legs. Quickly, his uncle straddled its shoulders, yanked its head to one side, and jammed the tool into its ear canal. An eerie silence wailed in the black air. Tlaloc gagged up a wad of phlegm and hocked it to the floor. He looked up when he heard his uncle howling at Animal, "Hit the damn thing! Hit it!"

Animal's eyes scanned the perimeter for something to use. He grabbed an old tire rim and lifted it high into the air and brought it down quick, crushing the pig's skull into an oblong shape. Blood sprayed across the garage like a punctured aerosol can. Animal lifted the rim up and again sent it slamming down. The beast's jaw clattered uncontrollably. "No!" Tlaloc shouted, wondering where the voice came from. The pig shivered and then quit struggling and plummeted onto its side.

Tlaloc curled against the back wall of the garage. His uncle was lying on the ground, a few feet away from the pig. He caught his breath, and then slowly rose to his feet and made his way toward the back of the garage. He lifted a mop from the ground and walked over to Tlaloc. "Here," he said, handing it to him. "Get cleaning."

The Ashes

Concerning a filial grandson

She had a way with her hands. They were always in motion.
Like birds in constant flight. Her hands had picked grapes and
pruned vines, pulled weeds and gripped handles. Were burned on
many a comal and wood estufa. Had pulled triggers and been rattled by hunting rifles. They had been used to plant gardens and
slap the disrespect out of any child. Back in the early forties, her
hands were used to shield her from rocks thrown by the white
boys of her south Texas youth. And then in the sixties used again
for the same purpose, in the fields of California and Wyoming. By
the time the eighties rolled around, her hands had accumulated
callus leather at least an inch thick from fingertip to palm. But
even with all this my grandmother still managed to take care of us.
When my father split and didn't tell a soul where he was going,
she took Mom and me in.

Most days when Mom worked, I stayed home with Grandma,
sedated by marathons of *M.A.S.H.* and *Guiding Light*. Sometimes
we would file through her boxes of clothes and trinkets that she
was preparing for a yard sale, other times we ended up pulling
weeds in her tomato garden, or doing the laundry in a large tin

bucket in the front yard. Always with a cigarette dangling from her lips. Sometimes the ash would get so long it would break off and scatter in the breeze. Otherwise she usually kept the ashes in a can, and when it was filled about halfway she would have me knead.them into the soil of her tomatoes. In a separate can is where she tossed all the cigarette butts. When she had a good collection of them she'd boil them in a large pot, and the entire house would fill with a stink that usually took weeks to settle. When the concoction cooled she would take out the butts and fill a spray bottle with it and use it as a pesticide for her garden. And she never used an ashtray, because that would be too easy. Instead, she dropped ashes right in the palm of her hand, until they gathered into a small mound. Then, she would tell me to open my mouth and feed them to me. "It will clean you out," she promised. I had no reason to doubt her. She was forever working her limpias on me. To heal me before any bit of darkness could settle in and take hold.

It bloomed in her left breast right around the time I was going into sixth grade. It was summer and I was supposed to start soccer that June, but instead got stuck with caring for my grandmother. Mom would drive her way out to Fresno for blasts of chemotherapy, and always she would come out of the clinic looking frailer than when she went in.

The first thing I noticed different were her fingers. They had shrunk. And then her face sunk, and her hair began to thin out. I could see the soft wrinkles of her scalp, specked with birthmarks and pocks. But she never wrapped her head in scarves or hats, like some of the other women at the clinic did.

Once, she had me accompany her to Neli's Beauty Shop so
that Frank could give her a trim. Despite having little of anything
left on her head, she continued to see the same hairdresser she
had for the last twenty-two years.

At first Frank did what he always did when she walked
through the door. He looked over his bifocals and shook his head.
"I was wondering when jew'd bless us with jour presence again,
Estelita," and then he would open his arms up and give her a kiss
on the cheek. Grandma wasn't much for affection, especially not
in public, but she always let Frank get away with it. "Look at jew.
Looks like jew lost some weight," Frank remarked. Grandma
didn't respond.

"Esque está enamorada," another hairdresser standing nearby
replied.

"That right, Estelita, jew in love?" Frank asked.

Grandma just rolled her eyes and smiled.

Frank sat her down in the reclining chair and pulled her head
back over the plastic headrest. The whole time Grandma kept to
herself, not saying much, letting Frank do his job as he went
about studying her sparse locks. Usually, it was impossible to shut
Frank up. His mouth did more slicing than his scissors. But today
you could tell there was something wrong. He slowly rinsed
Grandma's hair with a short hose, and picked through it with his
fingertips like he was separating beans. I sat near the radio and
watched as he did this. "Jew can change the station if jew want to,
mijo," he said, nodding at me. I fiddled with the knobs. The whole
time Grandma's eyes were shut and I could see her chest rise and
fall with each breath.

"Women have died for hair like this, Estelita," Frank once

said. "Diosito blessed jew with good hair genes. I mean look at all that black. It would make a raven jealous." But today he was light on the compliments.

As he pulled at her scalp he shook his head. And then he lifted his hands up from the wash basin, and with it a clump of hair. He rinsed it down the drain, and went back to rinsing, and then a few minutes later another clump. Grandma kept her eyes shut, but she was awake. I could tell because her fingertips were jumping to the beat of the song. Frank looked over his bifocals at the dead hair, and then glanced in my direction. I turned my head and pretended not to notice. He looked over at the other hairdresser. The woman frowned and shook her head. Frank gently ran his hands over Grandma's wet scalp again, and when he brought it up, another thick tuft gave away. He washed the locks down the drain quickly, and then took his glasses off and turned away. "Crystal Blue Persuasion" came on the radio and I turned it up a little and bobbed my head and glanced out the window. Frank put his glasses back on and squatted down next to Grandma, and then whispered something into her ear. She looked over at me and pulled up a limp smile.

By the time he had it all blown dry and styled up in a bob, her hair looked like nothing more than a nylon net pulled over complete baldness. She paid Frank and then let him kiss her cheek again, and just like that we were on our way home.

That afternoon, after Grandma and I shared a bowl of moyejas on her front porch, she showed me the cut across her chest. "You'll have to learn to help me clean it," she said, unbuttoning her gown just enough to give me a peek at the stitched wound. The skin was a deep red and swelled between the threading. The stitching itself was thick and coarse and looked like a baseball mitt unraveled. It started at her collarbone and tore down to her ribcage.

Later that night I'd dream about the gash. But it wasn't Grandma, it was the earth. The ground had cracked open and was pulling me in. I could feel a force trying to suck me into the hole as it grew and ate up everything in our neighborhood. I could see our house toppling into the gorge. Cars and pets and mailboxes, all of it, pouring in. I tried to run away from it but it was as if my legs were stuck in molasses. I couldn't pump them fast enough. The tear in the dirt widened and before I could get away I felt myself falling.

I awoke the next morning to Grandma calling for me from the kitchen. When I got there she already had a bucket of warm salt water and a bag of cotton balls on the table.

"Mijo," she said, "it needs to be cleaned." Her face was gray and she looked like she hadn't slept all night.

"Are you sure?" I asked, stalling.

She nodded her head and pointed to the rag in the bucket.

"Apaga la televisión," she said.

I went into the living room and shut it off. There, next to the sofa, was the trash can half-filled with yesterday's chicken gizzards and other bits of bile. I grabbed the can and went outside and tossed it into the garbage and went back in the house.

"Donde fuiste?" she asked.

"To throw out the trash," I said, dunking the rag into the salt water and ringing it out.

She pulled open her gown slightly. "Clean it just like I told you," she said. "The water first. Get it all over the cut."

I wrung the rag out over the wound and she shut her eyes tightly. "Keep going," she said. "Así." I soaked the rag again and again wrung it out on the cut. "The cotton," she said, "ándale." I dropped the rag into the bucket and grabbed a handful of cotton balls off the table. "Just like I taught you. Dab it. Así, mijo," she said, grabbing my wrist and moving my hand steadily over her skin. "No tengas miedo. It's got to be done right."

"It's getting stuck to the cut," I said.

She looked down and saw hundreds of little strands of cotton clinging to the stitches. "Take those pieces off," she said, "with your fingers."

I dried my hands on my pants and began to pluck each little fiber off with the tips of my fingernails. Grandma cringed and clamped her eyes shut.

When we were done, I put everything away and went outside and sat on the porch. It was still morning and the sun hadn't even reached the halfway point. I knew Mom wouldn't be home from work for several hours. Only when the sun was behind the headless palm tree at the end of the street was she almost here. But this didn't stop me from hoping that she might get off early.

It had been two days since I last cleaned her. I now had the routine down to only four minutes. Start to finish. Yesterday, she spent most of the time hanging over her bed vomiting into a bucket. Meanwhile, I ran around the house turning up the air conditioner, and then the heater, and then back to the air conditioner. All day long I listened to the neighbor kids play stickball out front and kept thinking to myself, just as soon as I do this one last chore. But the chores never stopped coming. The day before that, she went for another round of chemotherapy and then came home and crashed all afternoon.

While Grandma slept, the thought of her cut nagged me. I went into her room and took a close look at her. Her chest was rising and falling, barely. Through her hair I could see that her speckled scalp was sweating. I turned up the air conditioner full blast and pulled the sheet off her body. Her legs were sticking out from her gown and the ankles were bone white. I bundled the sheet up around her feet and up to her knees. I touched her forehead because that's what I had seen my mom do before—the skin was on fire.

Outside, the kids were pulling tricks on their skateboards and I could hear their wheels scraping across the pavement. "Do it," one said to the other, "I dare you." I went over to the window and watched them. Both boys were about my age. One of them was standing on the hood of a parked car. "And if I do it?" he asked. The other kid looked around. He saw me through the window and nodded.

I shut the curtains and went back to the bed. I looked down at her wrinkled face, and then peeled her gown back slowly and bent over for a close look. The gash was blackened and the skin around the left half of her chest was pink and risen like dough. The stitching looked like it was on the verge of bursting. I leaned in closer and caught the foul smell of rotting meat. I put my hand over my nose and mouth and leaned closer still, until my eyes were inches from her chest. Except for the swelling, and a small piece of loose thread imbedded right in the center of the wound itself, everything looked the same. I decided she needed another cleaning, and began preparing the salt water and rags and cotton balls. When I returned with the stuff, Grandma was just as I had left her. Her gown was still opened up and the cut exposed. The kids had stopped skating outside, and except for Grandma's wind chimes made of cans, the neighborhood was quiet again. I placed the rag into the water just as she had taught me and quietly wrung it out into the bucket. I leaned in close, inches away, but just as I was about to begin dabbing I noticed it looked different from before. Something was missing. It was the loose piece of thread. I touched the stitching gently to see if it had lodged itself in the cut, but nothing. I leaned closer still, until my eyelashes were practically skimming the surface of her missing breast, and rotated my eyeball left to right to find the lost piece. This is when I saw it. It was the exact same color of the thread, a bland white, but it moved. I jerked my head back and readjusted my eyes. It moved again. I poked it with my finger and it began writhing in place. A maggot. I froze for a second. And then ran to the bathroom got tweezers and ran back. By then the maggot had started to burrow its head back into the slit. I plucked its tail with the tweezers and I must've pressed too hard because half its body broke off and landed in the center of her chest. I snatched it up with my bare hands and chucked it to the floor and smashed it with my shoe. I flung the tweezers into the bucket of water, and then covered my mouth to stifle a scream that was coming on like a train.

That evening, when Mom came home, she took me outside on the porch and asked me how my day went. I wanted to tell her about the maggot I had found in Grandma's chest. But I didn't know how to say it. Every time I pictured it in my head I would wince and choke up. Mom fidgeted with her purse straps and looked out over the front yard. Then, she moved closer to me. I could smell her perfume. It was sweet and pungent. She lifted her hand and put it on my knee. "Summer's almost over, mijo," she said. "Ya merito."

Within a couple of weeks after the maggot incident, Grandma was gone. She had a fever that no medicine or remedio could cool off. Not even when Grandpa dunked her naked sagging body into a tub filled with cold water and ice, just like the doctor had told him to do, was she curable. The infection, the doctor said, was too severe.

In the following days, a few people brought over food and condolences in the form of enchilada casseroles or frijoles de la olla. Some would stay and pray the rosary. Others would help out by doing the dishes and taking some of Grandpa's dirty work shirts home with them to clean. A few even offered some money to help pay for the burial, but Grandpa refused, saying there would be no burial. Grandma was going to be cremated, just like she had wanted. After that revelation, except for family, visitors suddenly stopped coming over. And then everything went back to how it was before. Quiet.

One Sunday morning we took Grandma's ashes to the church to be blessed by Father Perez, but he refused. "It would be an abomination," he said.

"But she was here every Sunday," Mom pleaded. "Listening to your sermons. Confessing everything."

"Giving the church money," Grandpa interrupted. "Money she didn't have."

It didn't matter. Rules were rules.

And so we took Grandma home with us, in an urn that Mom and I had made from a coffee can. No holy water. No blessings from the church. It was the same can she used to gather her cigarette ashes in.

Powell, Wyoming

1979

Concerning early migrations in a boy's life

In Wyoming, during those rare weekends when Mom and the rest of the family didn't have to hoe sugar beets, we spent mornings at the dump yard in nearby Cody. My grandfather would park the truck alongside the road and we'd walk the short distance onto the grounds, and begin scavenging. Mom was forever on the lookout for dresses and cooking utensils, and once in awhile trinkets that she liked but knew she'd never buy in any store. Most of the stuff we picked up was broken, but a lot of it was fixable, according to the old campesino, and so we took it.

While the adults were busy wading through trash, me, Arturín, and Jacky would do some searching of our own. Arturín was usually looking for baseball equipment. One time he found a catcher's mitt that was in decent condition, and wouldn't take the thing off his hand for at least a month. He went all over town with it on. Flinging rocks up into the air and trying to catch them, but with little success. One time he chucked a fat dirt clod and when it came down it cracked open on the top of my head. I cried and

Arturín got his ass beat for it. He decided he was going to be a baseball player, and every time we went to the dump yard he hunted down all the pieces he needed to make this so. Jacky was too small back then to have that kind of devotion to anything. She mostly tagged along because that's what the younger ones do.

One time I found a stack of books that were partially wet, and even though I couldn't read them, I colored on the pages and made up stories and shared them with whoever was in the room. I did this until all the books were filled. By the end of the week Mom had thrown them out because they started getting moldy. The next day Grandpa found them in the trash bin and decided they'd make good kindling for the bonfire.

On other days, we'd spend the long hours sledding. Early on, Grandpa had shown us how a slick piece of cardboard made for a good time. He climbed atop the mountain of junk and sat down on it and then pushed himself off, and down he went. It wasn't fast enough for any real excitement, but at least it moved and that was always better than standing still. Besides a jagged pipe sticking out from the rubble now and then, the only thing we had to watch out for was that we didn't cross into the territory that everyone had deemed off limits.

A large section of the dump yard was used as a cemetery for dead cattle. "Watcha con los cebones," the old campesino would say, the worthless cattle. Bloated Jerseys with their bellies swollen and all four legs pointing up to the sky. They stunk up the air something sickening. Vultures and fattened crows scuttled around, pecking at the hard flesh. It was a combination of old blood and decay, and once in awhile if the sun was especially brutal, you would hear a loud pop and find entrails splattered for yards. They were forever warning us not to go near them. They told us stories about kids who didn't listen and wound up blind.

Whenever the cull count grew abundant, the dump yard manager bulldozed them into one big pile, doused them with gasoline, and lit them on fire. When this happened, we stopped what we were doing and hiked back up the bluff and waited it out. On the hood of my grandfather's pickup truck, we ate grapefruit and watched. Always there were hundreds of tiny explosions and guts and globs of shit flying in all directions. Arturín and I would think it cool, but Mom would say, "That's enough. Let's go home."

Driving away, Arturín and I stared out the back of the truck bed and watched the black smoke curl up into clouds. Depending on which way the wind blew that day, it either followed us into town or stretched itself out across the plains. Whenever Grandpa sensed our concern he reminded us that the culls' ashes were necessary, and that farmers spread them over the land to enrich the soil.

Those were the days that got spoiled.

On days that didn't, we finished scavenging early and then headed over to the Buffalo Bill Museum. It was a big house made up of giant logs way out in the middle of nowhere. Once in awhile a tour bus stopped by and dozens of people spilled out, snapping pictures and forming endless lines near the rest rooms. But most times it was only us, and a few tired locals who had the run of it. Mom always had me stand next to the statue of Buffalo Bill, toy tomahawk in hand, and pretend like I was taking him on. And then she would snap photos of me there, feeling like an idiot in front of strange onlookers. Meanwhile, the old campesino struck deals with the Indian dude who sold his jewelry out front. He had been a customer of the Indio's ever since he started coming to Wyoming for work—long before I was born. And because he knew

about loyalty the Indio always hooked him up. Once, when the
small nugget of gold embedded in the turquoise watch he bought
fell out, the Indio took it home with him and installed another
nugget in it free of charge. After that, Grandpa refused to buy jewelry from anyone else.

Later, we sat out in the parking lot and ate bologna sandwiches with ketchup and thought back on the day. Always we felt
lucky to be someplace else other than Catela. The air here was
thinner and tasted different. The mountains that loomed over that
part of Wyoming weren't like those rolling strips of pale yellow
that enclosed the valley. These were silver and jagged, and in
some places even touched the clouds. They were royal and
seemed important in ways that the ones hanging over Catela never
would. Plus, once in awhile you could spot a moose grazing along
the side of the road.

But then just as quick as sugar beet season came, it went.
Soon, we were packing Grandpa's truck with our belongings,
forced to leave behind what little junk we accumulated from the
dump yard that wouldn't fit. Arturín, Jacky, and I made our little
bed inside the truck's camper shell and nestled in for the long
drive back to the valley. We always left at night. Why? I don't
know. I only know that the sky was so clear at night we could see
every last star glittering at us from beyond. And then, like always,
we would wake up someplace else.

Bread

Concerning the culture of dough

Jesus calls it panocha, and every time he says this I laugh out loud.

"Isn't there another name for it?" I ask.

"No." He shakes his head, waving the triangle clump of brown in the air. "It's called panocha. Just panocha. It's what my dad calls it. It's what his dad called it. And it's what everyone who works in this panaderia calls it. Panocha."

I laugh and a piece of snot flies out of my nose.

"That's gross." Jesus says. "If you wanna work here you can't be laughing every time someone says panocha. I mean, what if my dad says, hey Tlaloc, get me some panocha. What are you gonna do then, huh? Just laugh at my dad? I'm serious, Loc. You gotta be cool, he takes his business very serious."

"Would that be the panocha business?"

"You fucker," he says, tossing a clump of panocha at my head.

Because I'm only twelve I get paid in pan dulce, and once in awhile, if Jesus's dad has it, cash. I don't mind the arrangement. Besides, summer around here is like living in Death Valley. Ain't shit to do except put your lips together and whistle.

Jesus and I met in P.E. when we both discovered we hated our names. His name isn't pronounced Heh-soos, like all the other kids named Jesus in Catela. Nah, it's pronounced just like the Son of God himself, Geez-us. At first, people have a problem with saying his name when they hear it's not Heh-soos, but Geez-us. But after awhile it grows on people and suddenly they're using it more than they have to.

One time a woman walked in and ordered two dozen bolillos, and when she left I heard her say to him, "Thank God your father owns this panaderia, Geez-us," and she pulled her rosary from between her cleavage, like a bucket out of the well, and kissed it and sent it back down into the hole. And just like that she walked out with her bag of bolillos, as if she'd gotten out of a confessional and dumped a week's worth of guilt on him. Jesus thought it was funny. He said people talk to him much differently when they learn that he's not just another panadero's son, but also the son of a Jewish carpenter.

Horacio is the dough kneader. A big man who if I eat too much pan dulce, says Jesus's dad, I will end up looking like. Horacio flips him the bird and continues to pound away at a wad of bread the size of a baby lamb.

"Órale, Horacio, no sudes en la masa," Jesus's dad tells him.

Horacio wipes the sheet of sweat from his forehead with his apron and is now punching the dough brutally.

Jesus says Horacio is like a third cousin of the family, or something like that. No one really knows how he's related, but one day, homeboy just showed up at their doorstep in tears, saying he'd been looking for them for years now, and that he made the trek all the way from Tijuana.

"Tijuana isn't that far," I say to Jesus.

"I know, but my mom couldn't turn him away. And since then he's been living in a shed behind our house. Calls my mom prima and everything, like he's known us his whole life. My mom tries making it okay by convincing herself that she slightly remembers him. It's in the back of my head, como un sueño, she says. It's been about five years now, so even if Horacio's not family by blood, he's guilty by association. And over there is Ebenezer," he says, pointing to a short man with red eyes. Ebenezer grins. His front teeth are capped silver. "Ebenezer just got back from Matamoros," Jesus whispers. "Got his teeth fixed. Took him three years but he saved up and went for it."

Ebenezer and Horacio stare at me like I'm a field mouse caught in a shoebox. Jesus tosses me an apron, then peels open a can of brown glaze and shows me how to properly spread it on a maple bar. "It only takes one scoop. See here?" he says, lathering with one stroke of the spatula. "One more time. Watch." He pulls another bar from a rack and does it again.

"I got it," I say. He hands me the spatula and I dunk it into the brown glaze and smear it across the bar. It looks like a giant mud paddy.

"You'll get the hang of it," he says, and gets to work.

The first few weeks go by easy. At eight o'clock each morning I ride my bike out to Jesus's house, and together we cruise about a mile up the road to the bakery. Sometimes, we roll along the ditch bank near the grapevines and pluck a handful of unripened grapes and eat them just like that. Raw and tart and crunchy with dirt. Other times we hang on to them until we reach the bakery, and then we drown them in vinegar and salt and eat them until our stomachs turn. Jesus's dad says we'll get worms if we keep eating them like that, but we know it's just something he says to keep us away from the grape fields.

When Jesus was younger, a farmer caught him stealing an eggplant and blasted him with a shotgun. The gun was loaded with rock salt, and it nailed Jesus on the back. By the next day his body had swelled like an inner tube from water retention. His mother had to prick him with sewing needles to drain him out. She saved the water in mason jars, like a lot of mothers around here do, and boiled it clean to water her tomatoes. Meanwhile, Jesus's scars grew into a constellation of a python slithering from his left shoulder blade all the way down to his butt crack.

"What the hell were you doing with an eggplant?" I once asked him.

"I don't know, it just looked like something cool to have."

"An eggplant?"

"I never ate one before, and thought I would take it home to my mom."

"Couldn't you just ask her to buy one?"

"I did. She never heard of an eggplant. She thought I was lying. 'There's no such thing as a plant that has eggs, menso!' That's what she said."

Most days are spent wrist-deep in chocolate bars and donuts, glazing. But now and then I'll powder an empanada or add coconut to a concha. During lunch breaks I stuff my face with warm bolillos, gutted and filled with refried beans. Then afterwards, I eat a few tortugas and wash it all down with warm Pepsi then get back to work. When four o'clock comes around, Jesus and I race our bikes out to the canal and dip our feet in the thin stream of water that winds its way down from the mountains and manages to trickle into Catela.

Ebenezer hardly ever says a word, just flashes his sparkling grill and laughs a lot. He's older than old and doesn't care about much anymore, except for making bread, and his daughter who lives in Canada. He is usually the first to arrive in the morning. He gets the ovens going and turns on the radio and listens to oldies. Even though he barely speaks English, he sings along.

Sissteen candles/ een my heart we glow

For eber 'n eber / I lub jew so / jess I lub jew soooo

This morning Jesus's dad orders me to ride along with Horacio and sell bread to the neighborhoods. We load up the van and we're out in the streets by six-thirty. We start on the east side of town, near the foothills, where we hit up one of the farmers. We don't even have to honk the horn. He already knows Horacio and recognizes the hum of the engine and is outside waiting. He is a tall thin white man, and wears sunglasses too dark to see his eyes. Horacio knows what he wants and tells me to fill a bag with twenty bizcochos. I do, and then hand it to the guy through the window and he passes me back a ten. "Keep the change," he says, but Horacio steals it from my grip.

Next, we meet up with a roach coach in the parking lot of an abandoned gas station. In thickly painted letters, the words "Tacos Galactico" are printed on the bumper.

"Wait here," Horacio says. "This'll take a couple of minutes."

I roll my window down and get the warm smell of chorizo that spews from the coach out onto the streets. Horacio slaps five with one of the men and the guy hands him a brown bag. Horacio peeks inside the bag then shuts it and makes his way back to the van.

"What was that about?" I ask.

"Lonche." He wads up the bag and stuffs it under his seat.

On the north side of town, where the old track houses are being restored, we rally up a crew of construction workers and unload an entire shelf of bread. They chomp away beneath their hard hats, thanking us, then slip back among stacks of used lumber and busted plastic pipes.

Next, we hit the south end of town, honking up and down the tired blocks until a few people straggle out and hand us their wilted bills and loose change. Horacio feels lucky when a half-lonely housewife hits on him. She's wearing a jogging suit and has her wiry hair pinned back in a ponytail. She says something about his working hands and wavy hair. He puts an extra piece of bread in her bag. Even though he pretends to know about women, he can only smile and grunt, then shy away by shifting bread around to make it look like he's busy.

Block after block it's more of the same thing. A few measly bucks here, a few there. Most of the times parents send their kids out. They come picking lint and pennies from their pockets, trying to make deals or score freebies. Once in awhile Horacio will give up a concha to the scrawniest of the bunch, telling his friends they better not bully him for it, or else.

"Or else, what?" the friends say.

"Los mato, carajos."

"You gotta catch us first, gordo!" One shouts, and they all laugh and run off barefoot down the hot street.

At noon we pull the truck beneath the shade of a tree and eat our burritos. Horacio reaches behind my seat and pulls out two cans of Coors. He hands me one and ignores me as he cracks his open and stuffs his mouth and drinks away. I tap the top of my can, like I had seen my dad do many times before, then crack it open. I bite my burrito, and then slowly lift the can to my mouth. I can feel Horacio looking at me from the corner of his eye. For a moment I hesitate, thinking it's some kind of test. But then he continues to eat and drink, and so do I. A half hour later I've got a buzz going. And just when I think it's coming to an end, Horacio opens the glove box and pulls out a bag of herb. He opens and sniffs it, then rolls a joint. He checks the side-view mirrors, belches, and then lights up. Even though I have been around it enough times to know exactly what to do, I have never smoked it. He swigs the rest of his beer, coughs, then passes it to me. I hit the joint and start puffing away and gagging like a pro. His heavy red eyes glare at me and smile, and I sit still waiting for something cool to happen. He hits the joint again, over and over, until most of the van is clouded in smoke, then passes it to me once more. I feel my neck wobble and relax, and I lift the joint to my lips and take a light drag, then pass it back. Horacio reaches in the glove box and pulls out a cassette tape. He jams it into the player and turns up the volume. A screaming trumpet cuts through the smoke and opens me up. He digs into his front pocket and passes me a small bottle of Visine. I dribble some into my eyes and it spills down my cheeks and shirt. He never says a word. Just sits there, staring off in his own world. It doesn't matter. The trumpet is doing all the talking.

"What is this?" I ask.

"Arturo Sandoval." His answer is quick and sharp. I look at the clock on the dashboard. It feels like we've been sitting here forever. At this point, I forget that I'm in a van half-empty with bread, in a part of Catela that doesn't look familiar to me. I look around for something recognizable, but everywhere dust devils are spinning and I can barely see past the silver goddess that adorns the hood of the van. Her wings are pinned back and she's flying in place, like a hummingbird in slow motion. Except she's sexier and curvier. Horacio clicks the ignition and the van chokes, and then leaps and turns on, and he laughs, and then I start laughing, and it's a long while before either of us can stop.

Eventually, we drive toward the south end of town, past the packing houses and grain silos. We turn down a narrow dirt road that leads through a field of persimmons and we stay on it for several miles. I have to take a piss so he pulls over and I get out and walk a little ways into the field. I unzip my pants, and can hear what sounds like a gang of birds screeching and flapping. I look over my head but no birds are there. I turn to my right, but all I see is Horacio's gargantuan arm hanging out of the van, waiting reluctantly. I look to my left and discover where the sound is coming from. It is a massive cage, the size of my bedroom. Its wire mesh is busting with all types of birds. Crows, swallowtails, ravens, they're all there, pouring over one another, snapping at feathers, shitting on heads, trying hard to squeeze through the wires. A few of the small ones make it. Others give up. And by the looks of it some get stuck and die like that. Wings pinned to their sides. Legs twisted at odd angles. Beaks and eyes eaten alive by merciless gangs of fire ants. There is no cage door. Horacio honks the horn and it echoes against the foothills. I zip up my pants and hurry back to the van.

It is four o'clock when we pull into Camp Renada. A no-man's land for anyone who doesn't work the farm upon which it sits. Everywhere are box homes and dilapidated trailers and tin sheds and whatever else a family can find shelter beneath. Sheets of cardboard are strewn sloppily over rooftops, on piles of dried grass, and around the busted-out windows of disemboweled cars. Cardboard and tin, tires and rims, and wire and rope keep the whole campito from flying off with the Pacific winds. If California were the estranged wealthy son who left and never returned, then Camp Renada would be the elderly arthritic mother from which he was born. Kids run about snot-nose wild, lassoing mocos around the perimeter like an imaginary fence meant to keep out intruders. Two little girls with pigtails and cock-eyed dolls are fleeing from a boy who's dangling a dead rat on the end of a stick and chasing after them. The others join in, until they spot our van bumping up the dirt path. They drop everything and go running.

"El Panadero!"

I see a smile pull over Horacio's face and for the first time all day I think he's not such an ogre after all. He honks the horn, until everyone has stopped what they are doing to see what the commotion is about.

An old woman comes out from behind a trailer and hobbles toward the van. She puffs on a hand-rolled cigarette and calls to Horacio.

"Ey, flaco. Dame tres cochinitos."

"Sí, señora," he replies, his eyes still bloodshot and glassy. She hands him her change and asks if it is enough. He counts it, then stares at me, and then back at the old lady. "Está bien." The woman grabs her bread and begins to head back when a swarm of

kids rushes past and nearly knocks her over. "Cabrones," she calls
out. The kids ignore her and begin hounding us for candies.

Horacio turns his pockets inside out but only wadded paper
and a few coins jingle. "Sorry, no tengo dulces hoy," he says, "pero
tengo galletitas." They stare at one another and nod their heads.
He jams a handful of sugar cookies into a bag and chucks it at
them. A short, stocky man is next in line. His face is shadowed by
a wide-brimmed hat.

"Q-vo!" he shouts. Horacio replies with a head nod. "No see
jew in tree weeks," says the man.

"Trabajando, como siempre," Horacio replies. "Y usted?"

The man takes his hat off and scratches his thinning hair.
"Buscando trabajo."

"Buscando?"

"Se acabó la pizca."

"Why you staying here then?" asks Horacio. "Porqué no jala pá
Washington?"

The man fans his fingers. "No hay plata," he says, squinting
into the sun. There is a long silence. Even the kids have quieted
to eat their cookies.

Horacio piles what's left of our bread into a bag until it nearly
spills over. "Buena suerte con eso, don," he says, placing the bag
into the man's arms.

"Estás seguro?" asks the man. "Jew chure?"

Horacio doesn't blink. He waves the man away and tells me to
get back in the van. "Que Dios lo bendiga," he shouts, turning the
ignition. Two toddlers with sagging diapers waddle up to the old
man, and all three stand there, watching us rumble off in a trail of
dust.

Hunting

1986

Concerning hairpin triggers at age twelve

I

It's Saturday morning, ten o'clock, when Jesus and I meet up with Zeta. He's got his dad's .22-caliber and a whole box of acorn shooters, the slimmest and fastest bullets around. According to Zeta, they're so accurate his dad once shot the wing off a mosquito.

Of course we know this is bullshit because Zeta's dad's eyeglasses are as thick as ice cubes, not to mention he's an alcoholic and his hands won't stop shaking.

We start out like always. Climbing over the big fence that blocks off the whole neighborhood from the train tracks. Because it's his dad's gun, Zeta goes first. Jesus and I are bloodhounds. We see something in the brush, something with hair, or fur, or whiskers, and we circle it until Zeta has a clean shot. Usually he misses. Usually we all miss. But sometimes we don't.

Near the tracks we spot a sofa that someone dumped. It's wet from last week's storm, but we check it out anyway. Sometimes, when we come across junk like this, stuff that people once used, we dissect the thing piece by piece. Like one time we found an orange crate filled with old clothes. But at that bottom of all that shit was a landmine of porno mags. The good stuff too. *Snatch. Hustler. Poonany.* Centerfolds with scratch-'n-sniff. We stuck them in a plastic bag and buried them beneath a rail tie. Only we know it's there.

This time we aren't so lucky. The sofa doesn't have anything worthwhile like this. We lift it up and find a family of opossums hiding out. The mother's got twenty babies sucking on her tits and she hisses at us. The babies look like miniature fetuses with fat tails and white peach fuzz. Their eyes are like pomegranate seeds. The father gets off his lazy ass and waddles off. The mother tries to inch her way toward a hole in the ground but the babies are too heavy for her. She turns and hisses, shows us her long teeth. Zeta points the .22 at her open mouth. And then, he blasts her head open. The babies are clueless. They keep sucking. All twenty of them. And then we take turns plucking them off one by one.

2

The sun is directly above us, and we're starving. For the last hour or so we've been pulling stone fruit off whatever tree comes our way. Plums. Peaches. Nectarines. It's enough. We want meat. I think about the pack of weenies I wanted to bring, but Zeta and Jesus thought it a stupid move. "Real hunters don't eat weenies," Zeta said. "They eat buffalo and shit like that," Jesus co-signed. So the plan is to catch our lunch. This is why Jesus's backpack is filled with matches and aluminum foil, and why Zeta has a stick of butter softening in his front pocket.

We're at the edge of the foothills, near the wind turbines. They're spinning over the groves and from this point we can look out over the treetops and see the haze that is Catela. We walk over the narrow bridge, to the other side of the irrigation canal. I call this place Garden of the Dogs. It's where Tio Alejandro brings our pets whenever they get sick, because we can't afford to take them to the vet. King is buried here. So are Coco and Piri. Even though Piri was a cat, she got along with Coco pretty well, so it made sense to bring her out here too. King was the first dog. He was bleeding from the mouth and ass when Tio brought us out here to bury him. He dug a hole and smashed the shovel blade against King's skull, and then threw dirt over him. Just like that. Coco was a different story. She had worms of some kind. Even though she looked cool on the outside, they were eating away at her guts and she looked too frail to be a rottweiler. But Coco didn't get the shovel. She just got left behind. Running after us in a cloud of dust. Her tongue hanging out so far she kept tripping over it and falling down and getting back up again, until she finally gave up and just stood there, watching us disappear into a needle point. I cried, but Tio told me it was the best thing for her. "Out here with all this land to run around on, what dog wouldn't want that?" he said. Piri wasn't sick or dead. His only problem was that he was a cat. Tio hated cats.

Jesus has the .22 now. He sets it down on the banks of the canal and climbs down near the water. Zeta and I follow him, balancing on rocks. "Over there," he says, pointing to a log that sits at the bottom of the narrow stream. I move to lift it and three orange shells scurry away. "There," he says, nudging Zeta. Zeta steps into the water and it rises just below his knees. He folds over and plunges his dirty hands down and grabs one. Its claw snaps his thumb and he flings it onto the embankment. "Another one," I shout, pointing near Zeta's feet. He slams his arm down into the water again and feels around for it, but comes up empty. Jesus climbs in and chases one upstream. "Over here," he shouts, "a shitload of them." Zeta and I hurry to where Jesus is at, and see that he's standing in pure orange. We walk and feel the crackle of shells beneath our shoes. They try to scatter but aren't fast enough. There's too many. We plunge our hands down and come up gold. We throw them onto the banks. And after a few minutes of this we climb out and begin counting our kill. Twenty-two.

While the guys separate the meat from the shells, I get the fire going. Zeta slaps a wad of butter on the aluminum foil, and when it gets to bubbling the crawdads go on.

We sit there on the shore of the canal, waiting for our meal. Jesus passes me the .22 and a handful of bullets. He shows me how to put them in the chamber and unlock the safety. Jokingly, I aim the barrel at his face and pull the trigger. He yells and punches me in the stomach. "Ever do that again and I swear to god I'll fuckin' kill you, puto." I'm not hungry anymore. Zeta looks at me and shakes his head. I don't care. I have the gun now. They can both kiss my ass. After they're done eating their share and mine, Jesus pulls a cigarette out of his sock and lights up.

"Where'd you get that from?" Zeta asks.

"My moms. She's got a whole box of them in her closet."

The guys share a few puffs, and then offer me a hit. I say fuck it and take a drag. The cherry glows and I suck until my lungs jerk and then cough everything up. They start laughing, and so do I. And now we're just three friends again, stuck in the middle of nowhere.

3

The bats are dancing over our heads, snapping at the insects that swarm in the dimming sunlight. We're headed back to the neighborhood. This is usually when shit happens. Last time out Zeta brought some of his mom's codeine pills. He swallowed them while on our way home and ended up shooting his foot. He aimed for the track rail and it ricocheted and caught him on the big toe. Now the thing looks like a chicharrón. It never healed right. The nail fell off and attempted to grow back, but it stopped about midway up the nail bed and shriveled into a brown knot. This is why he never wears chanclas in the summer. Or if he does, he wears them with socks.

We stop at the tracks for a few minutes because Jesus can't hold his shit any longer. All that crawdad got to him, and he's been farting for the last half hour. One long-ass blowhorn all the way down from the mountain. His face is white and he's walking funny. We pull out the bag of magazines and divvy them up, and everyone goes their own way.

I know it's the same orange tree because there's rocks piled everywhere. A few weeks ago we had been bombing the train with them and broke out all the windows. And when it stopped and the conductor came out after us we hid beneath this tree.

I sit down on a mattress of soft moldy leaves, the .22 by my side. The hideout smells like spoiled fruit and wet earth. I open the covers of *Snatch*, and staring back at me are the same tired faces I've been looking at since I was eleven. This was a year ago, and since then things have changed. My junk swells up to the size of King Kong every time I look at this stuff. The same titties. The same assholes. Same bush. I've seen it all at least a thousand times. But this time it's different.

I flip the pages, to the part where white boy is giving it to black girl, and dude couldn't look happier. I rub my junk and stare down hard at black girl. The dark hills of her thighs, I imagine them bumping up against my hips. Her long narrow body taking my bullet in its chamber. I hear Zeta calling out for Jesus and me. Jesus yells something back, but I keep my mouth shut, and keep rubbing and pulling. This must be what it feels like. Rubbing and pulling. Back and forth. On the next page, black girl has her mouth on white boy's junk. She's swallowing the thing whole, and he's got his eyes rolled back and looks like he's singing. I grip myself tight and pull hard. Over and over again, until it looks like what black girl is doing to white boy. I turn the page, and hear Jesus call out my name. My hand is pumping on its own now, like a jackhammer, the magazine is trembling. Black girl's open mouth is trembling too. White boy is singing all over the place. Jesus and Zeta call out. I grip it with all five fingers and squeeze tightly. My stomach warms. Black girl and white boy fall to the ground. Tighter still. The guys call out once more. And then, I pull the trigger.

The Legend of Adrastos

CIRCA 1887

Concerning the naming of a town and the effects of valley fever

The way I heard it, Adrastos dug his first hole when the temperature rose to a deadly one hundred and twenty-three, or as the people call it, el tenedor del Diablo. Peeking out through a veil of sweat, he jammed his spade into a crack and pried off earth chunk by chunk. Like this, it took him three mornings to break through two feet of hardpan and by the end of each day the skin on his arms, back, and face looked like it had been chewed up and spit out by El Demonio himself. There was no grand scheme behind his madness. He only intended to dig himself a hole where he could sleep in the cool without fear of a pack of dogs chewing off his ears in the middle of the night.

In the late afternoon, lying down in the small rut he had forged, he bit into a warm watermelon and thought about how he arrived at this place. Seed, juice, and pulp slithered down his neck and arms, and before it had a chance to settle on his skin it was sucked clean into the air. He watched it evaporate and leave a snake-like trace in the sand of his skin. When the stars made their appearance, he thought of home.

He missed the scent and feel of salty air on his stubbly face, and the way the seagulls cried and swooped down and skimmed sardine fat off the high tides. He missed the open Aegean Sea sprawled out beyond Chios Valley like a pale blue skirt flittering in the twirl of a woman's hips. He missed the broken streets and sticky nights drinking ouzo with his two brothers, overlooking their father's vineyard and talking of the inheritance to come.

"Us three will manage the vineyard, and each will get a third of the profits," they all agreed, throwing up their jiggers and slamming them back.

Adrastos could still clearly hear those words riding on the traitorous wind. The embarrassment of his stupidity huddled up on his cheeks and ignited a bonfire in his chest. Every time he thought of how his brothers had conspired against him he wanted to punch everything within arm's reach. A mosquito bit his lip, bringing him back to the loneliness of the valley, and to the barren patch of land he'd purchased with his last fifty dollars. He angrily swatted the insect off his face and in doing so cut his upper lip against his teeth.

According to his internal clock it was midnight. If the temperature cooled at all, he couldn't feel it. Every few hours a light breeze might flow past and lick the sweat off his body, but that was all. He stood knee high in the shallow rut and lifted the spade from the ground. Staring down into it he thought about the conversation he had with Chema, the man who sold him the land.

"This town used to be called Rosetta," Chema claimed. "Named after the first pioneer's wife. He was an Italiano, and the lady was a crazy woman from what I heard. Used to climb into the sack with any man that looked at her for more than two seconds," he said, squinting into the sun. "So one day she leaves the guy, up and went, no letter or nothing, just an empty closet and the scent of her perfume still in the air. A few months later the Italiano files papers and re-names the town Catela."

Adrastos shrugged his shoulders. "Catela?"

"Means *bitch* in the old Roman language."

Both men laughed, and then Adrastos grew a look of concern across his face. He wiped the sweat from his forehead and glanced down at the dirt. "And what about this land?"

"What about it?"

"Does it produce?"

"Boy, does it," Chema said, smirking.

"And the hardpan?"

"What—this?" Chema stomped the ground with the heel of his boot. "This is nothing. Just wait until the rain comes around again. You'll have more prime soil than you'll know what to do with."

Adrastos recalled the conversation while looking up at the full moon. It was whiter than ever and he could nearly see the craters from his place on earth. He let himself be taken by its clarity, and the longer he stared the more vivid it got. So entranced was he that after awhile he swore he could see Grecia in its reflective sheen.

In the distance, he spotted both brothers walking idly down rows of vineyard, smiling and fondling at the thick green leaves. One plucked at a vine and held two grapes the size of eggs in his clean hands. Together they plopped the grapes into their mouths and laughed. Adrastos knew they were laughing at him. His face contorted into a tangle of veins and he lifted the spade handle above his head and brought it down into the rut, smashing open a large stone. Sparks shot out around him as he continued bashing away at the earth. He went on like this for hours, until finally his legs gave away beneath him and he collapsed into the fresh grave.

The weeks flew past and still the monsoons hadn't come. Summer was nearly over, and fall was quickly on its way. By now, his hole was deeper than he was tall, and he had to dig himself a stairway to climb in and out. When he was away from the hole, he covered it with loose shrubs and tree branches.

One evening after returning from a long walk, he removed the shrubs and there at the bottom of his hole was an opossum. It looked as if it had been trapped there for hours. It was soiled in sweat and pathetically scratched at the dirt, but every time it got to the third or fourth step it fell back down. Adrastos startled the creature and it jumped onto its back and pretended to be dead. While it was lying there he took the opportunity to hit it with a rock and kill it for dinner. Later that night, as he sat by the fire laughing at just how delicious and tender opossum meat was, he thought it might be a good idea to dig another hole close by and use it for the sole purpose of trapping. He looked over at his trusty spade and in the light of the flames saw that its edges were blunted and worn. He needed a new one.

That night under the cloak of a moonless sky, he went to Chema's house and scoped out his toolshed. It was a shoddy piece of work, bound tightly with chicken wire and riddled with crooked nails. There was a lock on the door. Chickens clucked around the perimeter like nervous sentries. He eyed several spades hanging on the back wall. Most of them looked worn but one stood out. It was new and the blade was pristine. He shifted his eyes back and forth across the property. When all was clear, he wedged his old spade into the crack of the door and pried it open, slowly. It creaked and rattled the lock, and he froze. He pried again, this time quickly, until the lock snapped and rang out. He dropped onto the floor, and waited to see if the noise would wake the old man up but it didn't. He crept inside the shed, grabbed the new spade, and hurried back to his hole.

He examined the clean blade closely. It had been seventeen months since he had left Grecia. Five hundred and ten days since he last saw his own reflection. He stared at himself inside the blade and saw that his face, once healthy and fattened, had shriveled into a gaunt mask. His eyebrows were bushy and thick and looked as if a crow had spread its wings over his face. Both eyes were set deep in the sockets and brown half-moons hung beneath them. His teeth looked like kernels of corn.

Winter had passed and only a light smattering of rain had come and gone. It was barely enough to soften the soil, and within a few months he had forged himself a small cave several feet beneath the earth's surface. At one point he accidentally broke through the wall of his food trapper and now had himself a back door. He appreciated the spaciousness and decided he needed more of it.

During the spring months he plotted, and worked himself dumb, and by the end of summer the place looked like the underground city of Darinkuyu. The anatomy of the earth was pried open and exposed. Cavernous hallways revealed layers upon layers of sediment. Stacked atop animal bones and strange-shaped skulls, pieces of metal and curious stones. Mouse holes in all directions.

One morning he decided to go back up to the surface and check things out. He brought his spade along and walked the perimeters of his barren property. From this point of view, except for a few holes in the earth, one couldn't see that there was an entire renovation taking place beneath the surface.

Adrastos was feeling optimistic about the coming winter, and reasoned that the land was due for a downpour. He thought of how great it would be to finally plant some vegetables next spring and have some string beans to go with the rodents that fell into his trapper. He could taste a perfect meal on the tip of his tongue. He stabbed and smashed the spade head into the ground. Little spurts of dust rose in the heat. Mud caked around the corners of his mouth. He envisioned pulling a fat yam from the earth and shaking off its dirt and stuffing it raw between his teeth. The sweet starchiness of it going down into his stomach. Stab after stab he cursed the earth for not opening up. He tried in various spots, pissed into cracks to soften the soil, hammered away until he could no longer lift the spade. Defeated, he lowered himself down onto the valley floor, and then lying there did the only thing that came natural. He cried a despicable cry. The kind that no self-respecting Greco would be caught dead letting on. Until his tear ducts dried up and the vessels in both eyes burst. The pain forced his eyes shut. He squirmed onto his stomach and passed out cold.

Hours later, Adrastos awoke beneath the blinding glare of the sun. He blinked his eyes and decided to keep them shut. He felt around for his shovel, and when he found it he used it to heave himself up. Gaining his balance he planted one foot in front of the other and walked down into his hole. He was numb to the heat, and for that matter numb to the coolness. Minute by minute each one of his senses evaporated toward the sun, and eventually sound morphed into one long screaming stream of silence.

Adrastos bore deeper toward hell. And when he got there he made a left turn and burrowed sideways, away from Catela. He carved corners and forged random nooks. Back and forth, and in circles, down again, then up toward the surface. He tore through walls, connecting one room to the next. Quickly, because he knew it was only a matter of time before his eyes and hands expired for good. Then a hallway. Several hallways. Leading into each other. Leading nowhere. And then a thought occurred to him and he plunked both hands down into his seed stash and began scattering them aimlessly. Apricot and watermelon. Poking holes in the ceiling to let the sun in, the moon in. A window for the stars, a spy hole for intruders. Then a lemon tree. Peaches. An aquarium for the imaginary salmon. A terrarium of wolf spiders. A stable for the invisible horse carriage. A balcony for the romantic view of roots. Swollen and aromatic. Season after season, Adrastos clawed and fretted over his subterranean garden. Irrigation grooves trickled in. Seasons passed, and before long small green blades jutted up between his toes. Vines clawed their way out from the walls, searching for sunlight. Weeks later, an entanglement of foliage, knotted with buds and curious-looking petals opened and bloomed, and bore fruit, winding up through earth's ceiling. And when September reared its funny-shaped head like a turtle from its shell, Adrastos climbed the stairs toward the earth's surface. It had been over a year since last he stood on the level of the world. He swallowed hard the thick oxygen and went on up. Stumbling around with basket in hand he bent over and reached to pluck the first pick of his labors. Though he was half-blinded by the light, he could vividly see it in his mind's eye. It felt like nothing he'd ever held. He savored the feeling of all five fingertips grasping the pulpy flesh. He pulled a few more off the branch and set them in his basket. Made his way to the next tree and did the same. A wind rolled in and he knew by the smell of it that it was fall. He waited for the wind to pass and then walked back down into his hole.

Two

Ghosts of Tiburcio Vasquez

1991

Concerning the recipe for a perpetual fog

It's on the hood of Jesus's old beat-up truck. A pink rock
wound tightly in a piece of plastic. He untwists the plastic and
holds the rock between his dirty fingers. With a razor, he cuts it in
thin slices over a small mirror with the image of El Sagrado
Corazón printed on it. It's the kind of mirror you win your date at
the carnival hoping it's enough to get you laid, though usually it
isn't. When enough slices are splayed out, he chops the rock until
it becomes a fine powder, then sculpts four long rat tails. He pulls
a gutted ink pen from his coat, takes the pocketknife that dangles
from his key chain and cuts it in half to make a short straw.

"Here," he says, passing the straw. "Vuela."

My mouth curls up in one corner and I stare at it clueless.

"Vuela, man!" he says again, jamming the straw into my hand.

I lift it to my nose and hesitate.

"What? You ain't ever done cuca before?" He snatches the
straw from my grip. "Like this. Observe."

He puts it to his nose, bends over, and sucks up two lines in one long drag. He yanks his head back and pinches his nostrils, making a loud snorting sound. Without a word he passes the straw back to me. I angle it in my left nostril then lean over the mirror. Between the two thin lines I catch a glimpse of my reflection. Staring into the glare of both eyes, I shut them, then lean in close and inhale.

"Fuck!" I say, pawing at my nostrils to stop the burn.

Jesus laughs.

"Lean your head back and pinch your nose."

I try and end up sneezing. My eyes water. I wipe them and run both hands over my face. I lift my nose at him to make sure there aren't any flakes dangling from it.

"Am I good, man?"

"Yeah, cherry."

It's a shit-kickers' party on the outskirts of Woodlake. The town is pure hicksville. Nothing but pickup trucks and heaps of manure. On every front lawn, a glowing Santa or nativity scene. On our way here, we passed a house with a flashing baby Jesus, his little hand waving at passersby. "Órale, there I am," Jesus says, flipping himself the bird.

In the early twenties, Woodlake was a retreat for Catholic missionaries. This is what's left. The only reason we're here is because Jesus is trying to score with some cowgirl. He tells me she has friends, fine-ass chicks with horse-riding thighs. But even after a couple of hours have passed I'm still not able to settle into the scene like him.

The night is cold and wet. I see a ghostly blanket rolling in from the nearby almond fields and think of my grandfather, who used to claim that the fog was the wandering spirit of Tiburcio Vasquez, the Mexican hero whose body was dumped in the Tule Lake.

"You see," the old man would say, "the past is always working on you."

This is his way of telling me to stay clean.

Jesus and I stand around a bonfire for a few minutes, until our blood gets flowing again. I toss a tree limb into the flames and watch it rise. He's standing on the other side, his image half-blurred by the smoke, quietly sipping his beer. He smiles at me and bobs his head, thinking I'm paying attention to him, but I'm not. My mind is in the field behind him.

When I was five, my mother's boyfriend at the time left her and me stranded in a field in Wyoming. The sugar beet season had ended, and he was pissed off because she wasn't packed and ready to head back to California by the time he got off work. So, he loaded up the car and split. We lived in a mobile home ten miles from the nearest anything. My mom walked to the bus station with me in her arms, treading over endless rows of sugar beets. By the time we reached town everything was shut down, so we ducked into someone's backyard. It was a storage shed. We slept there until just before the sun cracked. When we reached the bus station that morning, one of the workers had recognized my mom and loaned her money for a bus ticket.

The image of her and me alone in that darkness does something to me. It stirs me up, and puts a surge in my chest, and now I feel like running. Without a word, my knees kick up and my heels begin digging into the soft earth. Jesus yells, "Where the fuck you going?" I don't answer. I can't. My thighs pump like pistons. I high-step fallen branches, gaining ground quickly. I can feel the white wetness of the fog moistening my clothes. My face dripping with it. I'm running blindly, expecting my eyes to adjust to the dark, but it never happens. Trusting the irrigation grooves beneath my feet, I step into a mud hole and fall to my knees. I rise up again and continue on. I can hear Jesus, his voice growing shallow. "Yo, Loc! Get your ass back here . . ." I don't stop. I run as far as my legs will carry me. I reach a small clearing, and begin swinging my arms wildly, jabbing at space, kicking and cussing. I reach down and grab a rock, two rocks, and fling them with everything I've got. They bounce off a tree trunk. One hits my foot. I break a branch off and snap it over my knee and begin to whip the invisible around me. I can hear it cutting through space. I clutch it like a shotgun and point up toward the moonless sky, firing one round after another. I can hear the blast echoing against the foothills. Each time I fire another shot, another opening in the blackness. Soon, a constellation of holes lights up the sky, and I feel as if I can breathe again.

When I return to the party I find Jesus inside the house. He's rolling joints for a circle of cowgirls. They're wasted and clawing at his thick arms for a hit. He's swooning them with stories of how he once worked for his uncle breaking horses in the mountains of Nuevo León. I hear him yakking about roping and getting bucked, and other cowboy talk I'm not familiar with. He pretends he's riding an invisible horse and flails about, spilling himself all over the girls. They giggle and blush and cozy up.

One of them, the fat one, gets up from the couch and makes her way toward me. Her face is caked with makeup and her sprawling tits are threatening the elastic on her halter top. "Hey, Efrain," she says, mistaking me for someone else. "Dude, I can't believe you're here."

I nod and smile, wondering how long she'd been waiting to jump ol' Efrain's bones. She saunters up close and looks me dead in the eye. We stand there for a second without saying anything. I can feel her hot drunk breath entering my nostrils. And then she attempts to spit in my face.

"What the fuck?" I say, but she's clueless.

Saliva dribbles down her chin and she tries to catch it before it falls onto her shirt. No luck. She slops it up with her long fingernail, wipes it on her pants, then laughs and staggers away.

I have to take a piss and decide to go looking for the bathroom. I find a door and open it. In the room, couples are tangled in the dark groping one another over a porn flick. "Shut the fucking door!" someone shouts. I swing my legs around and leave. I can tell my body's on the verge of giving out because I can hardly speak and my eyes are snapping photos that I won't remember. With my eyes half shut, I feel my way up the hall for the bathroom door. When I find it I fling my hose toward the hole in the toilet. Some of it manages to hit the target but most of it ends up on the linoleum and my shoes. My eyes get heavier, and for a quick moment I catch myself drifting off right there on the sink. I slam my eyelids open, cup my hand and drink some of that tasteless liquid. Something is different about this night. I shut my eyes to blink and forget to reopen them.

I'm in my Batman underwear tugging on Tio Alejandro's moustache. In one hand he's holding a cup of rompope, in the other, a gift. I want the gift. He gives it to me, but I can't open it.

The water runs ice cold. My eyes flutter open and I'm back at the sink. It lasts a few seconds. Then I'm out again.

Tio Alejandro is barricaded in a dark room. His little girl at his side tugs on his pants and begs him to make the cops go away. He tears off his shirt and leaves his tank top on to absorb the sweat. Wipes his face with the shirt and tosses it to the floor. Outside, a gang of cops is aimed and ready for him to make a move. They shout his name, plead with him to release the girl, but he has no intention of parting with her. The cops grow impatient, and so does Alejandro. In a desperate move he lunges across the living room past the opening in the curtains, toward the telephone. The bullet enters the window like a ray of light.

A loud blast rattles the walls and startles me back to the sink. The water is still running. I slop my hair back, and then shut it off. Out in the hallway, there is a brief moment of stillness, a glitch in the drunken air. Everyone's standing around petrified, wondering where it came from. Jesus finds me.

"We better get the fuck outta here," he says, pushing me from behind.

"Why? Wha . . . ?"

"Let's go, man . . ."

We hear voices shouting out back. A girl runs into the house with her face all twisted up. "Shelly!" she screams out.

Seconds later Shelly comes out of a room, pulling her skirt down and cussing. "Who the fuck? Goddammit!"

"Move, man, go!" Jesus says again, herding me toward the door.

Shelly flies past us and slams open the coat closet. She reaches in and yanks out a hunting rifle, then rushes out to the backyard. By now every last cowgirl is wasted and screaming her lungs off. Some idiots are heading out back to see what the fuck's going on, but not us. On our way out Jesus grabs an unattended bottle of tequila and stuffs it down the front of his pants. Before we reach the knob the door is jammed up with bodies. He muscles through, and then reaches back for me. I shrink myself and inch pass. We break through and are off and running up the dirt road to his truck. Another gunshot fires out and echoes against the foothills. Jesus's keys fall but I snatch them up. "You drive!" he yells at me. We jump into our seats and I floor it. The back end of his truck swings around and the tires screech as we bounce out onto the road.

"I don't know what the fuck was going on," he says, "but I wasn't 'bout to stay and find out, man."

"Did you see the size of that chick's gun?"

He looks at me and nods. "Bitch was pissed."

"Didn't even ask questions either, just up and got her gun."

"Just like that."

"Fucking Annie Oakley," Jesus says, and we both bust up laughing.

Catela is only four miles from Woodlake. On both sides of the road nothing but orange groves. It's a straight shot. I've driven these back roads so many times that I can do it blindfolded, drunk, and with my hands tied behind my back. Besides the oranges and maybe a few falling stars now and then, there is nothing else out here. Occasionally, you might spot a feral cat darting into a tree, or some half-dead abandoned dog clawing its way onto the asphalt. But other than that, it's just you and the blank.

Several minutes pass. Up the road, we spot two cop cars, and they rush past us blaring lights and sirens. Jesus turns to look back. For a second it looks as if they'll ignore us altogether, but then, from my rearview I see the red taillights glow.

"Shit," he says, "floor it, man. Go!"

I push my foot all the way down until it thunks, and the truck leaps and kicks off and I have to muscle the steering wheel to keep from losing control.

"We're about to get blamed for some shit," he says.

"What do you mean?"

"Did you see any other wetbacks at that party?"

"What the fuck you talking about?"

"Us, man, you and I. Woodlake ain't Catela . . ."

I check the rearview, and I can see headlights far off like a needle prick. Jesus jams his hand into his pocket and digs out his small bag of C. He bites it open.

"These motherfuckers will find any reason to bust a homeboy," he says. "There, turn there!" He points to a narrow opening in the orange grove. "Cut out the lights."

I follow his orders. "But we didn't do anything," I say.

He ignores me and looks back down the road where the head-lights are getting brighter.

"Whatever you do, man, drive slow so we don't kick up dust. That's the whole trick, bro."

He puts the leftover C into the palm of his hand and tosses the baggy out the window. I turn onto the dirt road.

"Dudes always fuck things up when they get all panicky and shit and try racing off like Dukes of Hazzard. Just take it easy, man. Zero dust."

I bring the truck to a near crawl as we slip between the orange trees.

"Slower," Jesus orders. "Don't fuck it up."

I look over my shoulder and see the headlights approaching quick.

"Whatever you do, Loc, don't hit the brakes. We're good man, just keep coasting."

We both roll our windows down and listen. Branches are snapping beneath our tires, and in the distance dogs are howling and barking their asses off. He turns his body half around and keeps his eyes glued to the street. As we slip further into the grove, I count the number of trees we pass, thinking if we could at least get to twenty. Twenty trees deep would hide us good enough.

"Fourteen . . . fifteen . . . ," I whisper to myself.

"Shhh." Jesus hushes me. "We gotta listen for the pig's car."

"Sixteen . . . seventeen . . ." I count in my head.

"There it is. I can hear it, man. He's coming."

"Eighteen . . . nineteen . . ."

"Here he comes . . . watch, he's gonna fly past, just watch his dumb ass."

I look into the rearview mirror. "Twenty . . . twenty-one . . ."

"C'mon," he says, his fingers nervously tapping the dashboard.

"Twenty-two . . . twenty-three . . ."

"Fuck. Where is he? C'mon . . ."

"Twenty-four . . . twenty—"

"There he is . . ."

A flash of light zips past the opening at the end of the row.

". . . and there he goes. The dumbass."

Jesus turns around and plops back into his seat. We both take a deep breath and relax. He stares down at the bulge in his crotch. I look down too, and then back up at him, and we both start laughing. He crams his hand down into his pants and pulls out the bottle of tequila. He lifts it to see the brand.

"Cazadores," he mumbles, unscrewing the cap and taking a long swig. He passes it to me. With one hand on the steering wheel I grab it and guzzle hard. Passing the bottle back and forth between us, we start the quiet road back to Catela.

The Rains Have Come and Cesar Chavez Is Dead

SPRING 1993

Concerning the dismemberment of an era

It is Monday afternoon and raining bullets but no one will remember this fact. Everyone's head is wrapped tightly around the news that Cesar Chavez is dead. On every channel and radio station, news bulletins interrupt regularly scheduled programs to kick down the details. Even the sound of traffic that wafts in from Highway 99, and the distant humming of tractors, and the barking dogs—all of it has stopped. There is no sound but the spill of rain gutters spewing from rooftops.

And just like that the central valley becomes the center of the universe. Politicians in Washington, D.C., issue broadcast condolences to Cesar's family. In Hollywood, Robert Redford appears on a news station and speaks about Cesar's life. Mexico jumps on the wagon too, showing old footage from early lettuce boycotts and endless marches. News anchormen receive reports of shockwaves from places like Lexington, Kentucky, and Chicago, and as far away as Peru and Stockholm. From their lips spill the names of all the towns I know well. Places like Wasco and Dinuba and Catela are mentioned. Panoramas of grape fields from Orosi, and packing plants in Orange Cove, and Sun Maid in Selma spill from the television onto our living room floor. I see flashes of landmarks I grew up around. There is the house made of bottles in Monson-Sultana. There is Yettem's old winery stinking up the open sky. And within a few hours Delano is drowning in media vans and high-powered cameras and satellite frequencies that fly out into space and back.

By five-thirty the next morning Highway 99 is a rippling sea of red huelga flags. Every sports car and lowrider and motorcycle and pickup truck flows south down the dogleg of this forgotten part of the Golden State. Battered work vans are jam-packed with campesinos peeking out tinted windows and waving red handkerchiefs and white flags and shouting out, "Que viva Mexico!" And we honk and wave and Zeta sticks his neck out the window and yells back, "Que viva marijuana!" And everyone busts up, except the highway patrol cruisers who are vulturing the whole convoy from nose to tail. But then it all comes to a dead stop. Right around Pixley, vehicles clot up and freeze, and it takes two long hours before our truck moves an inch. In that time, we pull our lawn chairs out and so do others, and now there's a mess of cockroaches scuttling out in the middle of the lanes and on the shoulders, playing cards and eating sandwiches and strumming guitars, making the best we can of the moment.

When we finally reach Delano, bodies are lined up into one infinite snake and it's flowing through the streets and between cracks and over fences. From our parking spot on a low bluff, the main road through town looks like a mudslide of adobe brown, an amoeba shifting and growing. None of us have ever seen anything

caught up in the middle of an intersection. The driver gets out
and begs people to move aside, but that's like asking a hurricane
to change directions. It ain't happening. The guy gives up and
throws his car in park and sits there, behind the wheel with his
head tossed back, while strange hands dance across the hood and
doors and windows of his car.

Zeta calls out, "Que viva los jalopies!" and a few others
respond, "Que viva!"

The guy laughs and lowers his windows and turns up his
music. Hips and shoulders begin to move and bounce and the
amoeba shifts directions again, and then lunges onward. The sun
is now leaning toward the Pacific Ocean, directly over Forty Acres,
and since we are coming in from the east side of Delano it sets in
the pupils of our eyes and blinds us for the last half mile. With
the sky now a toxic tangerine, and media helicopters swarming
around like field crows, the whole UFW headquarters has the
feeling of a dusty hallucination. People are gagging and breathing
it in, and waving for the pilots and camera crews to lay off. A
young guy with a thin moustache climbs onto a truck and spits
something indecipherable into a mega-bullhorn. He waves but it's
pointless. The cameras want the money shot.

An old man in a tattered tejana buckles in the swirling brown
cloud and falls to his knees. His hat goes flying off. And then
there are hands, young and old, reaching to lift him. And then his
hands extend up and he is pulled to his feet. His tired old face
breaks out into a smile.

It is in that tired face that I see my grandfather.

He was a big man. A shot caller among fruit pickers. His

moustache billowed out and hung down over both lips and scraped his chin. He wore a black tejana on his head to keep the sun from giving him paño. His shoulders were spread wide and his work boots reminded me of hooves the way they clopped up and down the wooden floor of his house. From his wrist clung a thick watch made of turquoise and silver that he purchased from an Indian friend in Wyoming.

Towards the end of it all he and I would sit out long afternoons, sucking down peppered moyejas, as he'd tell me stories about his life back in Texas. Beneath the shade of his grapefruit tree he'd reminisce about the early days, back when spics stayed on their side of town, and how thanks to segregation he ended up spending most of his young days playing near a pond.

My favorite story was the one where he and his brothers dove to the bottom of the pond and pulled out a handful of shiny white rocks. The rocks were so smooth and perfectly round that they used them for marbles, and after a few days, when the rocks were cracked and scuffed, they'd dive down into the lake and fish out more, pockets-full, he said.

"We didn't know what they were, we just wanted to play marbles. But then one day a teacher asked to see them. I handed him one and he looked at it. Let me see another, he said, and so I gave him another. He looked at us and asked us where we got them from. The pond we said. He asked if we had more and I said yeah, a whole bunch. They're at home, in a jar." My grandfather paused to stuff a gizzard into his mouth, and then continued. "So later that night there's a knock on our door, and it's the teacher. He wants to speak with my dad. They go out back and stay there for awhile. Finally my dad comes in and tells us to give him the marbles. We ask him, why? What did we do? But he doesn't say any-

thing, except, Give me the marbles! So we give him the jar. He
runs out back with the marbles and we don't see him or our
teacher the rest of the night. The next day we're at school and
right in the middle of class our dad walks in and tells the principal
he's taking us out for the day. But instead of home he takes us
shopping."

He took a gizzard from the bowl and plopped it into his
mouth. "Perlas," he says, pulling his thick glasses from his face
and wiping off the sweat with his flannel t-shirt. "Can you believe
that?"

Off and on it was like this, especially during the bleakest part
of the year, when all anyone in Catela could do was waste his or
her days getting stoned on *Roseanne* reruns. I always had plenty of
offers from the guys to go kick it by the tracks, but I was too
invested in the old campesino's stories. Besides, hanging with my
grandfather reminded me of those early days, back when my tios
and tias used to gather round the kitchen table and play poker all
night. Back when there was less on my mind, and the only thing I
needed to be happy was to hang out with my cousin Arturín and
chase the chickens from the neighbor's back yard.

On Friday nights, after an especially hard week of pulling
peaches, the old man would make the fattest, greasiest pot of
menudo, and invite the family over for a raucous marathon of
poker. Everyone started out on short bets, but after cartons of cig-
arettes were smoked and cases of Coors had been drunk, they
would start gambling their boot and bra savings. Sometimes it got
ugly, and someone (usually my Tia Bernadette) would accuse the
other (my Tio Alejandro) of holding cards, or some other "pinche

tranzas" he had going on. And then my mom would pull Alejandro outside to cool his head, and he'd confess to her how he was cheating, "but shit, Berni needs to be taught a lesson . . . and why does she always have to take shit to the next level like that?" And Mom would mellow him out, and they'd come back in, and before long they'd be dealing cards again. Meanwhile, the old campesino would be slipping me, Arturín, and Jacky dollar bills beneath the table, telling us not to forget him when we were rich.

By the time we reach Forty Acres it is late afternoon and the sun is cocked like a lazy eye. My legs are trembling from the eight-mile walk, and the skin on my forehead and back of my neck is neon pink. When a bead of sweat trickles down my scalp it stings. Where Jesus and Zeta are I don't know. I last saw them over an hour ago, when we crossed the highway overpass and they climbed the fence and started shouting some crazy shit at the cars passing below.

Before that, both of them had hooked up with some college chicks from Bakersfield and ducked into a gas station rest room to smoke a joint. They invited me but with all the cops swarming around, smoking weed would only put me in a bad trip, so I decided to pass. "Don't be a pussy, Loc," Jesus tried. "It's just one joint. And these chicks are hot, man."

"I'm cool," I said.

"Don't be like that."

"Fuck him," Zeta said, "Let's go. They ain't gonna wait around for our sorry asses."

Jesus turned his back to me and followed Zeta into the rest

room. After waiting around for too long, I said the hell with them
and went on my way.

Bodies are worn and the air between us is silent, except for
the shuffling of feet. People are struggling to catch their breath,
and find their friends in the loose mix. Hundreds of candles are lit
up and being passed around until the whole west side of Delano is
one long field of flickering seeds.

From where I stand, I can see Cesar's family, huddled up at
the front of the crowd. I make my way as close to the altar as I
can get. I want to see the man for myself. The little I know about
him can fill a thimble. I remember what my grandfather said, during one of our afternoons. I had asked him what he thought about
the farm workers' movement.

"I don't know," he replied, rubbing his forehead, "I was too
busy working."

The Chavez family says their goodbyes, and they're ushered to
a van. Now it's everyone else's turn. I get in line with the rest of
the crowd and wait. Jesus and Zeta are still lost, somewhere in
gringalandia. An hour passes and I'm finally within a few feet of
the coffin.

It is a plain box. No fancy brass knobs or decorations. No
wreaths or banners or flowers clinging to the side of it. Just a box.
Like something you'd put out back and chain your dog to. Faces
stare at it like all the magic has been sucked dry. Some people are
weeping, others are just there. Legs move forward and hands
reach out to touch the soft wood. The coffin is sealed shut, and a
photo of Cesar sits atop it. Fingertips are kissed and pressed
against the image. The photo is the same one you find everywhere. He looks about forty and is wearing a flannel shirt. A boy-

ish cowlick whips across his face. He is grinning. I approach the box, and get the faint smell of freshly cut wood. I look at the man standing next to me. His eyes are closed and he's gripping a small Bible, and little words are spilling from his mouth.

A year after Cesar's death, my grandfather began to fall apart, piece by piece. Not in that way people fall apart when some emotional shit happens that they can't handle. I mean his entire body had literally been parceled out.

At first it was the big toe on his right foot. Doctors told him it was jungle rot, the same kind soldiers develop if they've been in the trenches too long. The old campesino told them that the only trenches he'd ever been in were beneath the countless orange groves and endless grape fields of the San Joaquin Valley. Whatever the landscape, they said, it had to be cut off. He told them they were full of shit. It was a matter of insurance, he argued. If the toe was insured I bet you'd sure as hell find a way to let me keep it. And then several months later it was his left lung. They took a small cut of it for closer examination, fearing a cancerous speck that eventually turned out to be nothing more than a cyst. And can you put the piece back? he asked. Why would you want it back? they replied. Because it's mine and I don't want to get charged for it. He was out of the hospital for five weeks before he was forced to return again, but this time it was his stomach. He wasn't keeping down food, and so had to be admitted and fed nothing but liquids. This was the beginning of the end for him. A snip of his stomach was taken and scrutinized. Doctors kept expecting it to be cancer, and so did we, but it wasn't. Puzzled, they kept him there for several more weeks of observation. Days into his stay they took his teeth from him. He had worn dentures his whole adult life but now that his diet consisted solely of vegetarian cocktails, there was no need for teeth. And then he stopped smiling altogether. And then three weeks later, there it was. When we all had our backs turned to the possibility of death, cancer was busy blooming in his crotch like an undetected root. They reasoned with him all they could, explaining how much quality time he'd have left if they could just, delicately, just carefully, one quick snip, just, do away with his manhood. He told them to go fuck themselves this time, certain that if he had the right money, or if the piece of meat was insured they wouldn't even be having this conversation. Off it went.

After that, the whole of his skeleton shrunk several inches. He was hatless, and bootless, with nothing on except for an onion-skin-thin cloth that wavered in the breeze and bared his dark ass to the world whenever he turned on his side. Even his moustache had lost its volume.

I was sitting at the side of his bed, watching his chest rise and fall. It was autumn and raindrops were slapping the windows of his room. With both eyes shut he asked if I could help him up. He raised his hand slowly and I took it and pulled it across my shoulders and over my neck. I put my arm beneath his torso and tried lifting him up, but couldn't. I grabbed his other arm and placed it around my neck so that he clung to me like a little boy. His skin was loose and it hung over me like a robe. From this angle I was able to hoist him up enough so that he could sit at the edge of the bed.

"Up," he whispered into my ear. I muscled my arms around my grandfather and pulled on his torso, but it wouldn't budge. "Up," he mumbled again, and again I heaved, and again nothing.

Cradling him, we sat in silence for several minutes. I felt the nag of gravity calling his body back into the bed, and so I helped him, carefully. As soon as his head touched the pillow his body sighed—this was the last story I heard spill from the old campesino's mouth.

How to Catch a Train

It starts in the old man's liquor cabinet. Pour half the bottle of his expensive tequila into an empty container. Water down what's left and get out before he catches you in the act. At five in the afternoon wait at the corner for the guys. If Jesus can get it, they'll show up in his brother's El Camino. Otherwise, plan on them pulling up in Zeta's mom's Cadillac. It's a purple clunker, but if you slink far enough down into the seat, you can dodge all the eyes that stare at you like you've got some balls for riding in that tank.

The guys will arrive ten minutes late. Most likely they'll be stoned out of their minds. When they pull to the curb, a thread of herb will pour into your nostrils, and by the time you're in the back seat you'll be wearing the same stupid grin. When Zeta passes you the forty, throw it back into your mouth and let the gold liquid seep its way down your throat.

Before you reach the overpass that swerves down into Highway 99, you'll see a dirt road that leads to an abandoned barn. This is where you'll park so that you can all sit on the hood and avoid being seen by cops.

Pass the bottle around and guzzle away at those electric jolts that stab at your insides. You'll think it helps, and for a little bit, it does.

The train always arrives at ten minutes after six, so you want to be lying down on the tracks by then. If you're thinking too much about everything, that's okay. It's normal. Just ask yourself what else you got going on. Nothing, right?

Polish off the booze and let it take effect. Whatever happens, just keep your mouth shut. Otherwise, the guys will think you're a pussy. Even though they're feeling the same thing.

At a quarter till, you hike to the tracks, way out to where the bridge crosses over the highway. You'll know when you're getting close because of all the empty beer bottles lying around. Approaching the bridge you'll spot a half-deflated balloon flapping near the rail ties. It's anchored to a makeshift altar and a bouquet of wilted flowers. Close up you'll see the name NORMA scrawled on the cross-bar. A pocket-size class photo of her glued in the center. You bend down for a closer look, even though the guys are yelling at you to ignore it.

She's fine. About your age. Hair done up like in those girly magazines. Fingernails glossy like pimped-out lowriders. You know she spent at least half the day at Neli's Beauty Shop. Probably asked for the J-Lo special. You'll reach out to touch the weathered marks across her cheek, then lift the flowers gently and try wiping the mud off them, but it doesn't work. They're done for. Beneath them you'll find a muddy Ziploc bag filled with notes.

Just then, Jesus shouts at you to hurry up or you'll miss it. You pass on opening the bag and reading the letters, even though it burns you to find out what is in them.

When you reach the guys, Jesus will tell you the little he knows about Norma.

"Those notes are undelivered love letters to God," he'll say. "And they ain't never gonna reach him."

You have no idea what he means by this.

He'll go on. "When it happened, I heard it sounded like the train howled . . ."

"You're full of shit," Zeta will say.

But he'll continue, "and then there was a loud thud, like a golf club smacking a dirty rug."

That image makes you cringe, but you catch yourself and bulk back up, and before he can say another word, Zeta will spot the train in the distance.

"Let's go," he'll say, and the three of you will hurry to the tracks.

The bridge is an iron box welded down and dimpled with bolts. From end to end it stretches about eighty feet. From side to side, nine or ten. Just enough room to fit a single train and a few thin bodies, if done right. Jack-hammered scars line the insides where loose chains and rail spikes have gouged out chunks of wall and earth. Gnarled bolts, volcanic rock, and blades of glass litter the ground. On the walls, jagged graffiti, prayers, a poem.

You want to find a spot at the north end of the box, so if a chain is dangling from the train, it'll have been broken up before it gets to you. Whatever you do, don't lie down on the southern end or you'll come out with your face looking like moronga, nothing but a bloody clump. Once you find it, go ahead and clear the space out. Remove the rocks and glass and cigarette butts. Make yourself a comfortable nest. Ask yourself, if you had to sleep there for a night would it work. If the answer is yes, then you are ready, but if you're not sure then make it so that you are. There's still some calculation involved.

In a few minutes you'll spot the train like a dot on the horizon. From this point, it'll only be a matter of seconds before it all goes down. Here is your last chance to back out. But you won't do it because you're fully committed now and prove it by shutting both eyes and flexing your body into stone. Everyone is in their zone, and the only sound is the nervous breathing among the three of you. A crow will flutter down and startle you all. It'll perch itself on the rails for a split second, then fly away. You'll get the urge to raise your head to peek how close the train is, but quickly remember the cardinal rule of train catching—once you're in, stay in.

Your palms will begin to sweat, but no matter how tempting it is to wipe them, keep them pinned at your side, no exceptions. The most movement you can make is with your eyes and mouth. You can shout something at the guys, like, "Hey assholes, this is some crazy shit!" Nine out of ten times they won't shout back because they're concentrating too hard on not fucking up. Which is exactly what you should be doing.

Now you can hear the horn blowing a half mile away. The conductor does this whenever he approaches a bridge, a street, or any place he thinks pendejos might be lurking. It is a warning call that's meant to shake a person back into their senses. Ignore it. It isn't for you.

When the horn cuts out, count backwards from ten to one. By the time you reach five, everything including the wooden slats beneath the rails will want to jump out of its shell. You'll feel your body tense up. Let it. It's your anchor reflex. Even when your ass starts bouncing several inches off the earth, use your cheeks to grip the floor. Otherwise, you'll end up beneath the spinning guillotines.

When the tracks rumble and spit, you'll actually see the rails leaping into the air, and slapping down into the earth. Dust will fly up into your eyes. Turn your head away quickly, shut your mouth. It doesn't matter, your retinas will still sting like hell. In a hurricane of sparks, the train comes plowing through and enveloping everything in darkness. Like a starved lioness, she sharpens her claws against the flint of your stone stillness. A pebble snaps and bites you on the cheek. It burns and bleeds, and you hold back a howl and try listening for the end. But it's nowhere in sight. Just the grind of steel on steel, flashes of sparks beneath and above. One finds its way to your head and burns into the scalp. The smell of singed hair nearly rips you from your position but you hold. For a fleeting moment all is blur. It'll appear as if the train has slowed down to a silent crawl, and you can vividly see all the makings of it. The reinforced steel, welded crooks, and bound cables that run beneath it. The cargo door handles, the steps leading up to it. It all becomes clear, clear as a still pond. You consider standing up and stepping onto it. Here is your chance. It's now or never. But something bashes against your cage and more sparks spill all around you, and you awake from the daze and find it hasn't slowed down at all. You've been somewhere else completely. You open your mouth to scream and get the rusty fallout taste of rail spikes. You consider the dead flowers, the poem, and the hopeless balloon slumped at Norma's altar like a floating head. You wonder how long the letters in the Ziploc bag will go unread.

Norma's Lines

Concerning the inheritance of solteria

She comes from a long line of believers. All the way back to
her great-great abuela, Rosa Constante de Felix, or as everyone
referred to her, La Morena. Her mother never lets her forget that
behind those quick cumbia steps she's mastered since the age of
four, her hips, alma, y corazón run thick with sangre pura desde
Matanzas, Cuba. It's true. She's seen the photographs herself.

Once, when Norma was barely nine, her mother threw herself
a pity party after being denied (for the third time) a green card.
Present were a few neighbors, tias and their kids, and a dozen
stray dogs. After everyone had crashed out and nothing but spilled
bottles were left dancing on the empty floor, Norma's mother
lugged out the ragged suitcase from beneath her bed and filed
through the old photographs with her.

"See here," she said, pointing to a sepia photo of a teenage
girl. "This is your great abuela, Norma Hilda Gonzalez. This picture was taken around 1900. She's pretty, no?"

Even though she clearly had a moustache that rivaled any
man's, Norma nods politely and says, "Sí, 'amá, guapísima."

Next, her mother lifts out a warped black-and-white shot of an old woman and a young girl. "Who's this?" Norma asks.

"You don't recognize the girl?" her mother says, grinning sloppily from ear to ear. Her breath reeks of rum, but Norma doesn't mind because she rarely sees her smile these days and she'll take what she can get. She shakes her head. "Quién és?"

"That's me. When I was a little girl. And that's your abuela, when she was much younger too."

Her mother gets a faraway look in her eyes, and is nothing but a statue with her cold arm around Norma. She bends over and shuffles her fingers through the leaves of paper until she comes across a funny-looking woman dressed in tights and made up like a French ballerina. The photo itself looks as if it was snapped by a photographer on his first day of sobriety.

"Who's this?" she asks her mother.

Her mother snatches it from her hand and gazes into it, then shakes her head and laughs. "La Morena."

Here is where for the first time Norma is made aware that her great-great abuela, Rosa Constante de Felix, was a circus freak. Behind La Morena stands a deformed kid with fins for hands. A seal boy, just like the ones she's seen on PBS documentaries, whose legs were also attached mermaid-like at birth, and the only place anyone like that can turn to is a caravan of like-limbed bizarros who make a living and travel the world off their deformities. A massive beefy arm hangs over La Morena's shoulder and it belongs to the brick-headed muscle man who towers over the entire group of carnies. To the far left, squinting at La Morena with a fierce scowl, is a short woman with skin black as an orisha's kink, and an enormous bone pierced in one cheek and out the other. The whites of her eyes are haunting, and the pupils look as if they'll jump out of her skull and attack La Morena any second. She is clearly giving Norma's great-great abuela mal de ojo. But La Morena is poised. Because her only abnormalities are her gargantuan legs, muscular from years of tightrope walking, and her supple facial features. If she wasn't so dark, her mother once said, she'd look like one of those Russian matrioshka dolls. Norma has no idea what that is, but trusts that she is dead on.

"Why is that lady staring at her like that?" she asks.

Her mother doesn't tell her in that moment. Only mentions that it's way past her bedtime and shoos her off to her room. Norma stays up that night with the image of that bruja's eyes burned into her nine-year-old thoughts. And every time the house creaks on its own she swears it is her spirit coming to possess her. To distract herself, she thinks about the other photographs. Except for a few male cousins who were caught in the background doing some crazy shit like pinching their weenies, most of the people who populate her mother's old suitcase are women. Single women. She closes her eyes, content in knowing that her mother does not belong to this group, and for the time being, neither does she.

As a child Norma has spent time observing her mother and father, and how they aren't afraid of public displays of affection. The way he grabs her mother's face with both hands every time they kiss, or the way her voice changes and sounds light and airy when she replies to him in a loving manner. Sometimes, when the moment feels right, she wedges herself between their embrace like sandwich meat, and relishes their sloppy love. These moments are especially memorable, and she'll hang on to them dearly for the rest of her life.

But when her mom gets to arguing with her grandmother over

the phone about just how much love a woman can give a man before she loses herself completely and becomes nothing more than his esclava, Norma sees it in her mother's eyes, a hiccup of hesitation. As if for a nanosecond she considers her abuela's words. But then, thankfully, her mother recalls the three generations of uncommitted, loveless, and sexless women trapped in her suitcase. God forbid they try and put up a smile, or some hint of contentment long enough for a photograph to be taken. In the background, yards sunken and cluttered with dead things, flattened basketballs, car batteries, crow carcasses. Porches are nothing more than piles of sulking lumber infested with nails and splinters. In the kitchens, peeled linoleum and leaky faucets. In the living room, a warped velvet painting of La Virgen de Guadalupe, with the tiny cherub looking stepped on and defeated. All of this, evidence that whatever man once inhabited each of their lives, if only long enough to plant their seeds, was now nothing more than a memory. A bad one at that. Her mother thinks about all this. Norma thinks about all this. And early the next morning, while soaking in the bathtub before school, she clasps her small hands and thanks the sweet Lord for her mother and father, and all the shit they put up with in the name of love—in her name.

Right out of high school Norma and Lupe decide to move in together, and of course no one approves. Especially her mother.

"Hija, what are people gonna think when they see you two?" she says, packing on the guilt. Norma ignores her. "Catela is a small town," her mother continues. "Remember, people talk." But how could she ever forget. She's reminded every time her and Lupe hold hands in public.

Each morning she wakes up with her lover's warm breath spilling over her like a bucket of lechera. There is a sweet milkiness about it that she can't get enough of. Like clockwork, Lupe cooks breakfast for the two of them while she takes out the trash, and then they talk about what the day has in store. She complains to Lupe about how she can't stand working at the fruit packing plant with all the macho assholes cat-calling her non-stop, and how the shift manager just looks away and pretends to be deaf. And then Lupe tells her to quit and go back to school like she's always wanted, and for the hundredth time she has to explain why college isn't a good idea right now.

And then one day, as quickly as it started, it all comes to an end. Not like in *Love Story* where the love is intense and then one gets sick and dies and the other is there devoted until the last breath. Nothing like that.

Lupe is gone. Left Catela for good—according to the short note. Norma is alone. And in that loneliness she pulls out the suitcase that once belonged to her mother and father. One by one the pictures begin to make sense.

She glances over at a photo of her and Lupe that sits atop the television. Lupe is wearing a tank top and her supple shoulders shine from the hot lights of a flea market vendor. Norma is smiling, but Lupe's lips are barely lifted and her dark beautiful eyes seem to be saying something that only now, in the presence of all these photos of uncommitted, loveless, and sexless women, Norma is able to read. And in that moment, like a train wreck, it hits her. La Morena's blood isn't the only thing she has inherited.

The Pallbearer

Concerning this nonsense of redemption

One night, down Avenue 68, two cops saw a station wagon cruising through a stop sign and they followed it, lurking behind in the shadows. From where they were positioned a driver could not be seen and it appeared that the car was moving on its own. After running the stop sign it continued on to where the road ended, and bore right through a field of young plum trees, wiping out every thin sprig in its path until it hit an irrigation pipe and slammed to a halt. The cops turned their spotlight on and examined the vehicle from yards away. There was no movement inside. They got out of their cruiser and pulled their Glocks from their holsters. One shouted for the driver to come out, but no one did. They decided to call it in. When the third officer arrived, all three surrounded the car.

Which one of you got a look at the driver?" the third one whispered.

One and Two looked at each other. "Neither of us, sir," One replied.

Sir wiped a bead of sweat from his brow. Just then the car rocked slightly and they aimed their guns at it. One aimed for the steering wheel. Two at the passenger seat headrest. Sir pointed at the tires. "Come out, asshole," he yelled. The only reply was a farm dog yelping in the distance.

"Should we call in the canines?" One suggested.

"By the time they get here all the shit mighta hit the fan," Sir replied, returning to his vehicle. He pulled a vest from the trunk and strapped it on. "Just cover me, goddammit." Sir crouched low and duck-walked his way to the car.

When he approached the back window he hesitated and looked at his two men. Their eyes were fixed on him, waiting for a cue. He gripped his gun tight, then quickly stood up, aiming it into the vehicle. He squatted back down and shook his head. There was no one. He waddled around to the passenger door. The other two moved in closer to the rear. Sir gripped the car handle, and signaled again for his men to ready themselves. On the three count he took a deep breath and yanked the door open.

Lying on the floorboard were a set of legs. They were of course attached to a man's body. The man's head was tucked between the gearshift and the emergency brake. His eyes were half-open and white. In his left arm a syringe, still suckling from the vein like a parasite. He was out cold from a heavy dose of H.

They ransacked the vehicle and found a backpack crammed with junk—black tar, bombita, zoquete—you name it, he had it. According to the license in the man's wallet, his name was Arturín—Arturín Garza.

Back in the day, Arturín's mom would leave him and Jacky alone while she trekked to Mexico to "take care of business." Graciela would slap a few twenties down on the table, and drop some line like, "See you in a couple of days, and take care of your little sister." The first few times this happened, he actually counted the days, marked them on a calendar and everything. Figured by the time he crossed out Friday, she'd be opening the front door, bearing gifts. Of course this never happened. In the meantime, he and Jacky used to fight up a storm, over cartoons and food and who swiped the toy from the bottom of the cereal box and who didn't. They would leave each other purple and scarred, and even though Jacky was two years younger she'd always fuck him up good. Eventually, the money would run out, and they'd end up having to call Tio Alejandro or Grandpa to come pick them up.

By the time she was sixteen, Jacky had hitched up with some homeboy from Parlier, where she did the next logical thing and got pregnant. As for Arturín, he stayed in the streets doing what he did best. Hustling.

Holed up in an abandoned house behind Oval Liquor, he rigged the lights on, and kept a ball-peen hammer in his back pocket in case anybody tried fucking with him.

For awhile he cooked C, only because it was easy to make and sold like hotcakes. Nightly there'd be strange feet rustling the sycamore leaves behind the liquor store, ordering up baggies from a small hole he chipped away in the back room. Everybody, from squatters to hotties to Hmongitos and john-boys, was getting hooked up.

Aurelia was one of the regulars. She always showed up with her baby girl, Lesley, wrapped in her arms and gnawing on an old pacifier. Usually Aurelia paid up, but sometimes she was a little short, and Arturín would take pity on her and slide her some C at discount.

"Don't go fucking telling nobody 'bout this, Aurelia," he'd
make her promise.

"You know me, Art, I don't even know nobody in this fucked-
up town," she swore.

Aurelia had only been in Catela a short while. Came in on a
bus from Modesto, where she'd got into some trouble and decided
to move out here to live with her half-blind uncle. Turns out the
guy expected her to pay up in favors, so she took her little girl and
went looking for a remedy. When Arturín decided to expand the
operation, the first person he called on was Aurelia.

He'd fixed up a room for her and Lesley in the house. Even
put a padlock on their door so she could feel safe. And then he
taught her how to cook the best C around. The kind of shit that
had tweakers more loyal to them than to their own abuelitas. He
taught her how to strip the lithium from batteries, thin as onion
skin. How to keep the sulfuric acid from eating her flesh, and
getting in her blood. But most important, he taught her how to

stir the batter so that it didn't blow the whole place up.

"The best part," she once confessed to Arturín, "is I ain't gotta fuck with customers or numbers, or any of that stuff that always make me feel stupid."

To which Arturín had no reply.

It went on like this for nearly a year. They had a good thing going, and he was finally taking care of his own. He was wearing new tennis shoes now, and his pants were fitting him a little tighter these days. Once in awhile he'd take Aurelia to see a movie over at the Maya, and he even splurged on popcorn a couple of times, once with extra butter. But then as quickly as all good things in Catela come, they go.

He was returning from a sell in Orange Cove. It was the fattest deal of his short-lived career—nine ounces, no strings attached. He was already swimming in plans for the money when he found the cops shaking his place down. The dogs were barking like lunatics. The pulga was chopping up the night sky. He climbed up into the thick arms of the camphor tree at Oval Park and watched. It was late fall, the cold had teeth and the fog was rolling in. They ransacked everything. The cooking supplies were splayed out on the sidewalk. His clothes and equipment placed in large white bags. His windows were peeled open and the lights were on. Silhouettes of bodies stirred around the premises. He heard screaming, and then from behind the building Aurelia emerged. She was handcuffed and being dragged to a car.

"Lesley!" she cried out. Her voice had the rough growl of a tractor plowing hardpan. Sparks and screeches spilled from her mouth. "Fuckeen pigs!" She spat at the officers. Behind her, another cop was cradling a small bundle of blankets. Aurelia kicked the officer in the shin and then fell to the floor. He yanked her back up and threw her in the car. "Stupid cunt," he said, rubbing his leg. Arturín could see the pulga's searchlight illuminating the fog. He climbed higher up still, and then stuck both arms in his coat and wedged himself in the foliage, and thanked his lucky stars that there was no way they'd find his ass underneath the cloak of all that white.

A few years had passed, during which time only two random sightings of Arturín had been reported. Once at the flea market, washing car windows, and another time stumbling out of Intimo's in the early afternoon. And then when the old campesino died, Alejandro spent the entire day hunting Arturín down. He rolled in front of the Poverello House hoping to catch his nephew standing in the soup line, but no luck. He went to Intimo and asked the borrachos if they had seen him, but of course they all played dumb, and then hit him up for some change. One tecato tapped Alejandro's front pocket and got clocked on the forehead.

The next day, while driving past the park, he found Arturín sleeping beneath the tree. He parked across the street at Fiesta's Frosty Serve and ran over to him. Arturín's hair was shaggy, his body thinned out.

"Art," he said, nudging his leg with the tip of his boot. The body was limp. Alejandro squatted down and poked his nephew in the chest. "Art," he said again.

"Fuck off," Arturín replied, turning to squint into the sun.

"It's me. Your tio."

Arturín stared up at the tall figure above him until his eyes came into focus. Alejandro stood shaking his head. "Damn, you look like shit," he said.

Arturín rolled his body to the side and spat a brown wad into the dirt. He lifted his head and combed his fingers through his hair.

"You alright?"

"I'm good," he replied, hacking up a knot of phlegm.

When his head was clear of sleep he stared his uncle in the eye. A frayed silence hung between them. Alejandro looked away. He saw two guys come out of Oval Liquor with tallboys in hand. They stopped to light up a smoke before shuffling to the playground where they sat on the swings and cracked their beers open. He looked down at his watch, then over at his nephew.

"So what do you want?" Arturín asked.

Alejandro pulled the sunglasses off his face and hung them from his shirt collar.

He hooked his thumb on his belt loop and sighed. Arturín stood up and began dusting his pants off.

"It's your grandpa," Alejandro said, looking away.

"He sick?"

"Nah, he's. . . . well . . . fuck. He's gone, mijo."

Arturín looked down at the dirt and spat. He clicked his teeth and put both hands to his face and pulled the skin back and released.

"A few days ago."

"How'd it happen?"

"He never took care of himself, that's how."

"The fuck you mean?"

"You didn't know him, Art, I mean not like . . ." Alejandro hesitated. He scooped up some dirt and rubbed it between his palms "Shit, you know what? It don't matter. He's gone. That's it."

Arturín turned away and gazed out toward the street. The passing cars seemed to be standing still. "Now what?"

"His funeral's tomorrow."

"Where?"

"Smith Mountain."

Arturín pictured the sagging fence that surrounded the cemetery, and the small mountain itself casting a shadow over the grave markers. He always hated that cemetery, if only because towering over all those dead nobodies was a white mansionette, owned by the Trujillos, sitting fat like some obese kingdom high above Catela. The Trujillos were the only Mexicanos who could afford such an eyesore. Arturín always felt the place looked like a page out of some corny Spanish décor catalog. To top it off, it had a veranda that jutted so far out over the ledge that it looked as if the Trujillos were sticking their tongues out at those who could barely dream up such a luxury.

"Everyone's supposed to be there," Alejandro said.

"Who's everyone?"

"The family."

Arturín looked at him sideways and shook his head.

"I know it ain't easy, sobrino. I know you've been though some shit but. . . ." He paused. "You know she drove all the way from Deming to be here."

Arturín stood thinking. "Where's that?"

"It's in New Mexico, or El Paso, one of those."

Arturín bobbed his head.

"She wants to see you. She wanted to be the one to look for you too, but I told her it probably wasn't a good idea. That's why I'm here."

Arturín scratched at a mosquito bite behind his ear. He looked at his hand and saw an orange smear of blood. He wiped it on his shirt.

"Oh, another thing," Alejandro continued, "the family all talked about this, and we want you to be a pallbearer."

Arturín laughed. "Yeah right. A pallbearer." He shook his head.

"You and the rest of your cousins."

"And Tlaloc?" he asked, lifting an eyebrow.

"Said he'd be there. Also said he didn't think I'd find you."

The cars began moving again and rushing past. Arturín fidgeted with the ends of his moustache. "She really in town?"

"She's staying with a friend. Wants me to take you over there."

A string of crows flapped in the air above the tree, and then landed on a telephone wire. One barked at the other two and flew off. The two crows did nothing. They sat still, watching Arturín and Alejandro walk out from under the shadow of the tree.

Time away had aged her, but for the most part she looked good. Better than he had remembered her. Her face was round and her body jiggled. She wore heavy makeup on her eyes and cheekbones, and under the yellow lights of the restaurant Arturín could see the granules of powder.

The first several minutes he just sat there, drowning his eggs in ketchup and Tabasco sauce and forking them down quickly. The entire time his gargantuan moustache threatened to sweep the plate clean. Meanwhile, she smeared jelly on her toast and tried making polite conversation.

"So, what have you been up to?"

"Just grinding the stone," Arturín replied, tearing open his English muffin and slathering butter on it.

"Oh," she said, pretending to know what that meant.

He smacked his mouth when he chewed and gulped when he drank his water. She ignored it, and fiddled with the sugar dispenser.

"You thin, mijo," she said.

He sucked down a forkful of hash browns and washed it with a swig of black coffee. And then another gulp. And then more hash browns. She clicked her fingernails on the tabletop and shifted her eyes.

"I have to use the rest room," she said, scooting out of her seat.

He dusted the corners of his mouth with his napkin, then crumpled it in his hand and continued eating. She took a good look at him, then got up and walked off.

When she returned, his plate was wiped clean and he was crunching on ice. She sat down and started right in. "Look, I'm sorry . . ."

"Don't," he said, lifting his hand at her. Ice spilled from his mouth.

"Don't what?"

"Don't say anything about anything. It is what it is." He lifted his glass to his lips and a chunk of ice clinked against his teeth.

"Arturín," she continued, "If I could change things . . ."

"Don't sweat it . . . I said it is what it is."

"What does that mean? *It is what it is*, what's that?" she said, tossing her head back.

"It means, just leave it."

She looked away for a second, and the waiter arrived with the check. She pulled a credit card from her wallet and handed it to him and he hurried away. Arturín tore the plastic wrapper off a toothpick and wedged it between his teeth. Neither of them said a word for several minutes. He combed his moustache for food crumbs while she looked out the window toward the parking lot and sipped her coffee. The sun was rising up over the foothills and reflecting off the parked cars. She angled her face away from the glare, and then turned slowly and looked him in the eye. Arturín slouched further down in his seat. She pulled her sunglasses off her face and reached across the table, touching his hand with her fingertips. He didn't move it. They sat like this for a few seconds, until the waiter returned with her card.

On the way home they stopped at the Am-Vet Thrift Store and she bought him a used blazer for the funeral. He tried it on, and even though it was long on the arms, he liked it and wore it out the store.

In the passenger's seat he sat quiet and stared through the window, watching the streets, one by one, click past like hands on a clock. He remembered back to when he was a kid and thought she was the greatest mom in the whole goddamn universe, and how he'd bring her all kinds of crazy shit, like fallen leaves and rocks. And how for years she kept all that junk at the bottom of her underwear drawer, piling up until he'd find them in the trash one day. From the corner of his eye, he looked at his mom's hand resting on the steering wheel, the fake-gold rings and painted nails. He looked at her arm, and then followed it up to her elbow, and collarbone, and to her face. He saw her wilted eyes, that sad shade of brown, and for a brief moment, he felt sorry for her.

When the car turned in front of Oval Park he spotted the camphor tree. Standing beneath it was a woman. As the car moved closer he thought he was looking at a ghost. It was Aurelia, and she was alone. She stood there like a rag doll, resting the weight of her upper body on the ball of her hip. Her hair was much shorter than he remembered it.

As they drove passed he stared at her from the corner of his eye, wondering what she was doing back in Catela. It had been almost four years since the bust. The last he heard, she was on a fast track at Chowchilla Women's Penitentiary and had only spent a few months inside before she was released to some halfway house in nearby Madera. Lesley had been auctioned off to some rich family in Sacramento, and the last sighting of Aurelia was of her sucking off some fulano for a speck of H in Orange Cove.

When they got home, Arturín showered and readied himself for the funeral. He put on his new coat and folded back the cuffs, then slapped on his shoes and walked out into the living room. His mom looked at him and smiled. It felt good to see her smile and know that he was the reason for it.

"Looks nice," she said, taking a break from applying her mascara to say this.

He doused some hair gel into his hands and smeared it over his head. He put his hands in the sink and ran water over them. "I'm heading out for awhile," he said, wiping them dry on the inside of his coat.

"Oh?"

"Don't sweat it. I'll be back in time."

"It starts in two hours."

He nodded his head and opened the front door. She plopped her hands down in her lap and watched the door shut behind him.

Arturín ran to Fiesta's Frosty Serve and bought three cheeseburgers and a large Coke. He made his way to the park and found Aurelia. She was sitting beneath the tree unrolling a wad of paper napkins and blowing her nose into it.

"Aurelia."

She looked up. Arturín stepped closer.

"Motherfucker. Art?"

He smiled.

"Shit, look at you. Who died?" she chuckled, standing up to hug him.

He felt her bones hold his body in a weak grip, and took in the smell of cigarette smoke and dirty hair.

"I can't fuckeen believe this," she said, still hanging on.

Arturín pried her off and opened the bag. "I got you burgers."

Aurelia peeked inside and took a whiff. She grabbed the soda from his hand and sucked on the straw for a good minute. She stopped and burped, and then took another drink.

"Look, Aurelia, I don't have time. I gotta be at a funeral."

"No shit? Whose?" she asked, pulling the paper wrapper off a hamburger and stuffing it in her face.

"My grandfather."

She chewed the food down and took a drink of soda.

"I just wanted to bring you this." He set the bag down on the ground and readjusted the sleeves of his coat.

Aurelia leaned over and pulled a napkin from the bag.

"You look good," he said. "I mean, you know, the haircut and all, looks good on you."

She bit into the hamburger, looked him in the eyes, and took another drink. Some of it leaked out the side of her mouth, and she laughed and coughed out a piece of pickle, and it flew onto Arturín's coat.

"Damn, sorry 'bout that," she said, wiping it off.

"Don't worry 'bout it," he replied, looking over his shoulder to see if anyone was watching.

When they both sat down on the grass, Aurelia sidled up beside him and continued gnawing on her burger. Watching her pink cracked lips move up and down like that reminded him of when they first met. He remembers how she looked way too young to be hauling around a baby, and how her soft gaze was evidence that she still trusted the world way too much.

Arturín leaned over and kissed Aurelia on the neck. Food in her mouth, she closed her eyes and let her head fall back. He could taste the dirt on her skin and behind her ears, but it didn't stop him. Aurelia set her food down and stuffed her bony fingers between his legs and grabbed at his crotch. He stuck his cold hand up her shirt and felt her tired nipples bunched up like crinoline. He yanked at them and sucked on her ear. "It's been awhile," she mumbled, pulling down his zipper, and folding her body over his. A light wind rustled the leaves, and carried with it the harsh stink of melting tires and smoke and ash. It was a burn day and the farmers kept their bonfires fed with all the junk that accumulates on a farm. Specks of floating black landed on their clothes and skin. Arturín wanted to get up and move over to the rest rooms but Aurelia kept on, begging him to give it to her right then and there. He pulled his blazer off and used it to cover up. Aurelia shed her pants and pulled him into her, spreading her tiny hands all over his bumpy back. She felt just like he remembered, and despite the way she smelled like a bag of decaying trout out in the open like that, he was into her. Into her like he hadn't been into anything in a long time.

None of this actually happened. But he was certain that if he missed the funeral, this is exactly the kind of bullshit that would be on everyone's mind. This or some other type of tranzas. There was no sex. There was Aurelia at the park, and cheeseburgers, and Arturín. And then there were cops. While they ran Arturín's name through the system, he sat handcuffed, explaining.

"I'm supposed to be at the funeral of Felix Hernandez, Sr.," he said. "I'm a pallbearer."

"Fuck these assholes, Art," Aurelia shouted. "You don't owe them an explanation."

"Shut up," he yelled back at her. "Call the Smith Mountain cemetery," he continued, "you'll see."

Officer One walked back to his car and got on the radio. Arturín could see him moving his lips. "Got the time?" he asked Officer Two.

"It's a quarter past one."

Arturín's eyebrows knotted up. He looked out onto the street, expecting to see his mom's car drive past but the road was empty. He thought about the small moment they had shared during breakfast. The feeling of her fingertips on his skin was like ice and fire rolled into one. And then he thought about the funeral. He remembered what his uncle had told him, about how the old campesino had died, and that he was much better off in heaven than he ever was on earth. And then he thought about his cousin

Tlaloc, who he hadn't seen in over fifteen years. Tlaloc, the little shit who always fought with him. Tlaloc, who he raced down heaps of junk in a Wyoming that seemed like a separate life entirely. And now, here they both were, grown men, about to carry the old campesino's body in front of the family. He looked down at the lapels on his coat and fixed his eyes on the stitching.

Aurelia was still busy cussing at the cops. Officer Two got fed up and stuck her in the backseat of his cruiser. She was screaming some shit that no one except she could hear. Through the window her mouth looked like a big fat O. Arturín shook his head and stared at the dirty sky. He lowered his eyes and took another glance up the road. Suddenly, he saw his mom's car approaching in the distance. It caught him off guard and he looked away.

"You hiding from someone?" asked Officer Two.

Arturín didn't answer. He looked again and saw her getting closer. Her hair was fixed nicely and her sunglasses were pulled down over her face. The officer asked again. "You know that car?"

"Yeah, that's my ride," Arturín replied.

Both One and Two stared at the approaching car, and waited to see what it would do. Arturín lifted his head and whistled at her, but she was still too far away. He tried again, but again no luck. The officers looked at him and shook their heads. Arturín kept his eyes on the car. He whistled once more, this time louder. Aurelia was kicking at the window with her feet, and one of the officers ran over to shut her up.

"It's her," Arturín said, "my moms." He whistled and called out, "Graciela! 'Ama!"

"That's enough," said the officer.

"But it's her," he pleaded. "Swear to God, man."

The officer looked again at the woman in the car, and this

time Graciela looked in his direction. She slowed down and low-ered her sunglasses and Arturín felt a hint of relief rise in his chest. He folded over and let out a nervous chuckle. The officer fixed his gaze on the woman as she peered out over the landscape of Oval Park. Graciela angled her eyes at the two officers and then at her son. She looked Arturín up and down. At the secondhand blazer she'd bought for him just hours ago, and at the tightly rolled cuffs on his sleeves. She stared at his long black moustache and droopy eyes, and couldn't help but remember him as a child, with that same apologetic gaze on his face and untied shoelaces on his feet. She stared at her son. And he stared at her. And then he managed to lift up a smile. And then she did the only thing she knew how. Graciela lifted her sunglasses back over her face. Rolled up the window. And then steadily, hesitantly, applied pres-sure to the gas, and continued on toward the cemetery without him.

Antifaz

~~Hijo mio~~
~~I wish~~

~~Dear Tlaloc,~~
~~Many times I~~

Tlaloc,

In this picture I got in my head your about three. It's a nice
morning and were eating huaraches de flor de calabaza at a tianguis somewhere in Tijuana. It's you your mama and me. The food
is greasy but we hungry so they go down good. But then you pull
me by my wrist over to the dulces. Cocadas, higos en almíbar y
Pelon Pelo Ricos you want them all but your mama says only one.
She don't want to make you a diabetic she says but I buy you five
anyways. At first she gets made at me but then after she sees how
you are so happy she shakes her head and laughs. The way she
laughs that morning she reminds me of ~~this good thing~~ a little girl.
And then she asks me why Im looking at her like that. Like what I
say but she don't say nothing back except a smiles. I used to
always give her this look because she was so pretty. And then you
yank my arm to the pony-ride and your hands got almíbar all over

them so I have to lick your tiny fingers to get it off. I remember we can't get all your fingers because this tickles you too much. And then the ponies all looked sick but you didn't care cuz you still wanted to ride one. Please you begged us in your little voice so we got you on one and watched you go around in circles at least a hundred times. But then your mama went to see the flowers. She was forever into the flowers. When the man stopped the pony ride I pulled you off and you fell to sleep right on my shoulder. Your hands had horsehair stuck all over on them. I find your mama and shes got a miniature nopal in her hand, and shes got a look in her eyes. It was a pretty little thing with a bunch of tiny flowers all over it. I never seen a nopal like this she said. I can't believe these colors they're so beautiful. I can never forget the look in her eyes. And then she touches the petals of the flowers the same way she touches your face. And they say God don't exist. She always said stuff like this whenever she sees something pretty. I give her money to buy the nopalito and then she says shes going to give it to your abuela. This exactly what she needs. I really don't care what she was going to do with it all I care is that she's happy I tell her. She says she is.

But then ~~as usual~~ it all went to shit. It got late and we were all tired. I remember I was driving fast swerving in and out of traffic like crazy cuz I just wanted to get us home before dark. I was mad cuz your mama kept us at that the tianguis too long and Tijuana's such a dirty place. It look like every damn building was falling apart. On every corner a man or woman holding up a sign that says Tengo Sida. Or else they have no legs, or one eye, or pulling some other tranzas. It made me sick to look at. I told her all this

shit was not good for you to be around. Even the damn pigeons
there look like tecatos and then, I accidentally ran over some
maybe three. There feathers were stuck in the windshield wipers
and I turned the wipers on and they went flying in the air. Your
mama thinks I did this on purpose. This is how it got started.

Your such an asshole, she called me. This was her favorite
word for me back then. Your in the back seat of course quiet like
always. I look at you and you got this nasty antifaz pulled on your
eyes. ~~The car bangs over the potholes and~~ I am cussing at the road
and your mama yells at me something about the way I'm driving.
It must been one hundred degrees and the air conditioner didn't
work. We were all sweating like perros. Your damn tongue was
hung out your head and I said something to her about this and she
thinks Im calling you a dog and then she spits right at me. And
then you complain that your stomach hurts and makes this horri-
ble noise from your throat and then, you hold your stomach and
do this silent crying thing you always did. No tears or nothing like
that just a lot of shaking and then you shut your eyes. When your
mama sees you she gets more pissed off and grabs my hat and
throws it out the window. It hits the car behind us and now this
asshole is flipping me off and trying to pull me over. Look what
the fuck you did I says to her and I reach for the damn nopalito
that she cares so much about. She tries putting it on the floorboard between her legs but I'm swinging my arm around trying to
knock it out of her hands. She pulls one of the flowers off by acci-
dent and sees that it's stuck to a toothpick. Can you believe that?
A pinche toothpick. I bust out laughing at her and she pulls
another one and that one is also held on with a toothpick. Just
thinking about it makes me laugh right now. She keeps pulling the
little flowers out until there almost all gone. She got this sad look

on her face and I just keep laughing at her. And then you start crying out loud and your mama throws the nopalito out the window and then climbs over to the backseat to hold you: I look at her in the rearview mirror and she's giving me this look like she wished I was ~~invisible~~ dead. She might have given me this look before but for some reason I only notice it this one time. She got on the same loco antifaz you got except hers don't go away.

One time on your birthday when you were probably seven I drove ~~passed~~ by the old house to see you. I wanted to see you really badly but I don't know I guess too much stuff was in my mind so I didn't stop after all. Please dont think of me badly ~~no matter what~~. Anyways if your still reading this I wish I could tell you other stories Tlaloc. ~~The truth is~~ I got nothing. There are others but there all the same. In case you want to know where I been doing, Im living now in Brownsville Texas today. Maybe you could come and see me if you want to one day. I work in Corpus though where your abuela was born. My addreess is on the envelope. With this letter I am sending you a picture of me and you and your tio sitting on your abuela's front porch. Also I am sending you twenty dollars just so you can't never say that I gave you nothing even though I know that this isn't true.

~~Siempre,~~

Con respeto,

tu padre

~~ps: I went t~~

Windfallen

Concerning a mother and her son

"Tall-oak," a deep voice calls out. "Which one of you is Tall-oak?"

I shut my eyes hoping the voice goes away.

"Tall-oak. That you?" Something hits my foot and I manage to open my eyes.

"Let's go, you got paperwork."

I can see a pair of shiny black boots standing over me. Farther up is a gun holstered around a leather belt. A little higher still, a fat moustache, chomping on a piece of gum.

The moustache helps me to my feet and I follow him, stepping over the rest of the bodies sweating out the remains of last night's poison. The moustache stops above some güero, calls him Sweeney and yanks him up by the kid's soiled yellow hair. When Sweeney gets to his feet I see that he's pissed himself good, the entire front of his pants look a shade darker than the back. The moustache huffs and shoots me a look. Sweeney's purple eyes roll over in their sockets and when the blue pupils register and click back into place I recognize him. He doesn't know me. He wouldn't. But I know him. He's the son of a dairy farmer, lives up on Rocky Hill. Has something like a few brothers and sisters. A bunch of closet junkies, Jesus once told me. He said that one time he and his cousin Pepsi went up there to sell the dude some cuca, and that they paid crazy money for some shitty stuff that was more lithium than anything else.

"When he asked us why the rock was so pink, we told him it was some new shit called Energizer Bunny, and the pendejo fell for it," Jesus said. "Started grinding that shit right there in that big-ass patio of his. A fuckin' family affair too. All of them tweakers, swear to God. Even the little one, with her fine-ass eighth-grade body. Shoulda seen her hittin' that shit, like a goddamn pro. Pepsi wanted to stay and bang her but I told him he was outta his fuckin' mind. Those rednecks would hang his ass." Jesus went on. "When them fools got all nice and revved up and started playing beer games, me and Pepsi went into the kitchen and wiped those motherfuckers clean out, man. Took all kinds of shit. Cans of oysters, dried fruit, caviar, and head cheese—don't ask me what the fuck a head cheese is, I told Pepsi, but the motherfucker took it anyway." Jesus chuckled. "I'm sayin', no smart rico has any business living in Catela. Shit, no dumb rico for that matter."

Sweeney's wearing white shorts that hug his nuts and a floral print shirt with pink hibiscus flowers. Looks like a Hawaiian luau threw up on him. He's got a single flip-flop tucked into his back pocket and both his feet look like they've been treading through cow paddies all night. He retches and something green flies out of his mouth, and the moustache cusses at him for it.

He gets put into a room where a tall man in a brown suit is waiting for him. The door closes and the moustache walks me down the hall to a metal window where a large woman is sitting behind a stack of papers. She starts flipping through pages, talking orders and codes and spouting off things I "need to remember or else." It doesn't take long for all this to get to me, and I can taste the heat of alcohol from the night before. It's making its way up my throat, but I swallow it back down for the moment. When she's done, the moustache hands me a metal clipboard with numbers on it and tells me to stand against the wall. He snaps my picture and chuckles. "There's a winner," he says to the woman, and she laughs and her fat tits jiggle.

The ground is still wet with dew when I step out of the building. Mom is sitting in the car, her elbow on the steering wheel and her head in her hand, staring at me. The look on her face reminds me of the time I gave her a fake lotto ticket for her birthday. She almost dropped dead when she scratched off that third number and it read $250,000. Man, all she could do was tremble and cry. And then she started turning her head, back and forth, as if she was looking for something, as if she was taking inventory of all the small details of our lives. The lifted edges of the linoleum floor. The blackened stove and greasy kitchen walls. The way the curtains sagged like an old pair of testicles—all of it, running through her mind, and no words to describe the emotions. Grandpa thought Mom was having a nervous breakdown, so he snatched the ticket from her hand and looked at it, counted the numbers over and over again, out loud. And then his eyes welled up, and he wrapped his thick arms around her, and she let herself go, collapsing into his chest, crying.

The expression she's got right now is the exact same one she had when I told her the lotto ticket was a fake.

I get in the car and she doesn't say a word. Not for awhile at least. The sun is cruel this morning, and no matter what direction we're headed it is intent on keeping its eye on me. Mom cruises the car out toward Yettem, near the foothills, and then over by Woodlake. An hour later we reach the valley walls and she turns back and heads toward Orosi. Then Orange Cove. And then Reedley. Around three we stop for gas in Dinuba and then start heading back to Catela. When words finally come to her, we're floating down a back road that runs along a canal that stretches for miles.

"You think I'm mad at you," she finally says.

At first I think she's messing with me, like she's playing cool to get something out of me. Some piece of information that maybe the cops didn't know or didn't tell her. I shrug my shoulders.

"I'm not," she says, glancing in my direction.

I still don't say a word.

"I told the cops I didn't want to know what they had you in there for. Told them I didn't need to know. I already know."

I look at her from the corner of my eye.

She holds her gaze steady through the window and sighs. "I can smell it on you."

I hold myself back from shooting her a look, and pretend to stare out the window at the strawberry field where two small bodies are hunched over picking. I roll down the window and shield my eyes from the glare that comes from the long strip of water that makes up the canal. If she was pissed off at me I would know exactly what to do. I would open the car door and jump. But maybe she knows this about me.

"I've been here before, Tlaloc," she continues. "Been here *before* before." She pauses and concentrates on slowing the car down so that a truck hauling potatoes can pass. "You aren't the first man in my life, you know. Just the last one. Remember that." She rolls down her window and waves the trucker past and his trailer shakes and sidles up next to us for a minute before it cuts back into our lane. Mom wipes the corner of her eye with her thumb, and then closes her mouth and doesn't say another word.

It is now that I realize something about my mom I had never known. More than any word or iron or lamp she's ever thrown at me, her silence hits the hardest. I feel like I want to fold myself into my pocket and get lost with the lint.

Later that night I hear her crying in her room. She's trying to stifle her sobs with a pillow, but with the walls as thin as they are I hear almost everything. Her prayers. Her tiny whispered requests to God. To her own mother. To someone. I hear her little words, fading as the minutes pass. The last droplets of devotion, trickling out, like a leaky faucet.

And like always, I know they will go unanswered.

Three

Talina

1995

Concerning Armenia's lost daughter and the
sound of bells

Talina and I were never serious. We only saw each other now
and then to keep the hearth stoked. It wasn't about love, not for
me at least. She was twelve years older and had been through it
all. She only came around after it had been a week or two without
sex, or if shit got especially tough on her, like if her boss kept trying to get down her pants and wouldn't back off. Or if the memory
of her brother Armen kept slipping in and no drunk or high could
take it away.

Sometimes I wondered if the only reason she kept seeing me
was because I reminded her of him. We were both about the same
age. We both kept our hair somewhere between long and short,
and once, while at the flea market, I even got mistaken for him.
Sometimes we'd be right in the middle of fucking and she'd be
clawing at my back like she was digging for something. I know it
sounds crazy, but this shit does run through my mind now and
then.

We met at Jesus's little sister Ana's quince años bash. I hesitate to call it a quinceñiera because the church had nothing to do with this one. Everyone knew Jesus's sister wasn't about to go in front of no padre in a white garment and make-believe something that just wasn't true. By the time she was thirteen she was already laying down with guys twice her age. One time, I caught her and some fulano getting it on beneath a row of grapes. Right on the dirt, legs wide open and fulano humping away. She begged me to promise I wouldn't tell her brother, but of course, I did. She got her ass beat hard, once by Jesus, and then by her mother.

In Catela, wherever there's a wedding or some kind of special event going down, it's understood that people will show up, regardless of whether or not they were invited. If you really want a party to be private, you have to shell out some big bucks and rent a hall way out in Fresno.

At every party there's always two sections with two types of people. Invitados and leftovers. Invitados always get the tables with the decorations. Leftovers only get chairs, if they're lucky. Invitados get first dibs on food and dessert. Leftovers get the leftovers. When the live band kicks on, invitados have the run of the dance floor until the band's time is up. When the DJ starts spinning, now it is anybody's dance floor. And here comes the craziest part of it all. Leftovers are always the ones who stay behind after the party and pick up the mess. A few considerate invitados might hang around and help out, but mostly, it's the leftovers who do it all. And then they get to take home whatever leftovers are still around. Hence their name. This goes for cake, beer, lost earrings, wallets, cigarette packs, table centerpieces, all of it, up for grabs.

Talina was a leftover. If not for the fact that she didn't know anyone at the party, then for the simple fact that she was Armenian. I hadn't seen her around Catela before. Months later, when she told me that she was once married to a paisa, and they lived out in Yettem, I knew why.

I asked her to dance, and she accepted. All night we stood there, rocking back and forth, me grinding my belt buckle into her hips, and her thrusting back.

"You better slow down," she whispered, "it's a quinceñiera, not some brothel."

I pulled back a little. "I like you," I told her.

She smiled.

At that moment the disco ball flashed a beam across her face and I caught a glimpse of the crow's feet around her eyes. She knew right then that I was on to her age. She grabbed my hands and pushed them further down her ass, and this quickly took my attention away from her face.

After the party, we went back to her place. It was an attic room, above Pato's Carniceria, so the walls stunk like raw meat 24/7. It had a low slanted ceiling and only one window. From it you could see the bell at Holy Family Church, where every hour on the hour it rang.

"That's one of the reasons I love this little place," she said, "because the bells sound so pretty from here, don't you think?"

"They're alright," I replied, taking in the details.

Her sink was an old industrial-style wash basin, the kind you see in packing houses, with a big hole for a drain where all the shit of the day gets scraped into and goes down to some unknown cesspool beneath the earth. On top of a flimsy table were the milk crates she stored her dishes in. On the other side of the room, the toilet was tucked into a corner, where if not for a partition made of curtains it would have been out in the open. Her laundry was strewn over a thin rope that ran from the window to her front door. On it hung several blouses, a pair of panty hose, and two bras—one red and one almost transparent, the material was so thin. As for her bed, it was nothing more than two mattresses sandwiched on the middle of the floor.

"How can anyone not love the sound of bells," she asked out loud.

"What about alarm bells?"

"Alarms aren't bells," she said. "Alarms are just . . . well, they're alarms."

"Whatever," I said, grabbing her from behind and pulling her toward me.

"Why don't you tell me something about yourself," she asked, after a couple of hours of me not saying much. She threw her thigh over my body and propped her head on my bicep and snuggled up close. I shook my head.

"You shy?"

"Nah. Just nothing to say, I guess."

She sighed, and then got up and cracked us open a couple more beers and passed me one. I chugged mine and set the empty can down by the side of the bed. She went to turn on the radio. From behind, her bare ass fell flat and looked like a rumpled quesadilla when she walked. It reminded me that she was a woman. Radio Bilingüe was playing an Arturo Sandoval tribute, and Talina started to change it but I asked her to keep it on and so she did.

"You like this music?" she asked, settling back down into bed.

"It's cool. I like that there are no words. Sometimes words just fuck things up."

"You think so?"

A small silence bloomed between us.

"I like words in music," she said. "They describe what I feel. The shit I don't have words for, you know."

I nodded.

"Like when I hear Carole King, I think of my mother."

"She liked Carole King?"

"No, she never heard of Carole King, but that's the thing. Whenever I hear Carole sing 'So Far Away,' I feel like she must've known what it was like for my family to have come to the United States."

I nodded.

"Or like whenever I hear 'Before the Next Teardrop Falls,' I think of my ex. What a damn loser." She took a swig of beer.

"And what about reggaetón?" I asked her, jokingly.

Her eyes opened up and she gave me a blank look.

"What? Something wrong?"

She polished off her beer and dropped the can at the foot of the bed.

"What's up? You alright?"

She walked over to the toilet and sat down and peed, not even shutting the curtains.

"Sorry if I said something to piss you off."

"No, it's not a big deal," she said, flushing the toilet and making her way back to the bed. She lifted the covers up over her body and laid still. The church bell rang, and her mouth tilted into a fragile smile.

"My brother Armen used to listen to reggaetón. Man, I hated that shit, but he couldn't get enough of it. That stupid beat, those dumb lyrics. Couldn't even understand what they were saying half the time, but he fucking ate that shit up."

"How old is he?"

"He was twenty when they killed him."

I kept my mouth shut for a good long minute, feeling like an idiot.

"It's alright. It's been awhile now."

"How'd it happen?"

"Remember the shooting that happened at the flea a few years back? The one where some assholes shot a kid for dating their sister?"

"That was him?"

Talina nodded.

"That was fucked up."

"Yeah, it's alright now though. I mean, I'm alright now, at least. They caught the guys."

I didn't say a word. She turned on her side, away from me, and I listened to her breathing grow deeper and deeper.

The next morning we got dressed and I took her to breakfast at La Elegante. She had huevos rancheros and I went for the menudo. We ate until we got full and then went outside and crossed the street into Oval Park, where we sat beneath the cool morning sunlight and did nothing. The tecatos were nowhere in sight, but the paisas were out in full effect, slapping cards down on concrete benches and swilling tallboys in brown bags. Across the street, the Maxi Raspados cart already had a line of kids snaking around the palm trees, drooling over who was getting what flavor and how big. Mothers in saggy sweatpants and flip-flops were wiping mocos off the faces of infants. Three homeboys were dragging themselves out of a house and into a pickup truck, and then cruising off in a swell of hard banda.

Talina and I just laid there, with our backs to the earth and eyes to the canopy of leaves above, not saying or doing anything.

Just there, in the immense thickness of it all, like two sharp
blades of grass waiting to get stepped on.

Later, I walked her home, and left her on the sidewalk in front
of the carniceria, where we kissed good and long, until the linger-
ing stink of meat pulled us apart.

"I'll call you," I said.

"Don't worry about it," she replied, half-smiling and standing
there waving in the middle of a Catela afternoon.

Alejandro's Akashic

B. 1960

I

Alejandro moves toward Bernadette's bed. The curtains are drawn. An orange glow of dusk penetrates and floods the room. She is tangled up beneath her blankets. Only her head is visible, but he can't find her eyes beneath the web of hair. She's been crying.

"I hate playing this game, Berni," he says. "What the fuck's wrong with you?"

Bernadette doesn't reply.

Forty-five minutes drag past before her hand emerges from beneath the covers. A chipped acrylic nail pulls back enough hair to reveal her left eye.

"You gonna tell me or what?" he demands.

Her eye shuts, then reopens. Slowly, she glances down at her stomach, then back up at Alejandro. "I'm pregnant."

2

One year later, Alejandro's hovering over the kitchen table clutching a butcher knife.

"You fuckin' cunt!" he shouts.

"Fuck you! Son-of-a-bitch!" she fires back.

Jelly doesn't know what the words mean yet, but she sees the look on both their faces and begins to cry. Bernadette tightens her grip on Jelly, and with her free hand lifts the hot iron and takes a swing at Alejandro.

"See if I don't burn your eyes out, motherfucker!" she yells.

"Put the baby down, Berni!"

"Since when the fuck do you care about her?"

"Fuck you!"

"Fuck you!"

She chucks the iron at him and the cord whips Jelly's bare legs and she screams. Alejandro sends the knife flying through the window busting glass in all directions. Jelly's head jerks back and forth. He yanks at her arm and she cries out. Bernadette beats his grip loose and bites the part of his forearm where his tattoo reads Jelly's name. She spits at him and cusses something indecipherable, and her mouth looks like a big hole in her head and now Jelly can see right down into the pit of her stomach.

3

Four years have passed now. Alejandro sees Bernadette when it's his turn to keep Jelly. She's everything he ever wanted in a daughter. Flowing river of hair, skin like driftwood, a sweet little mouth puckered like a bird's beak. She runs to him, and her tiny voice chimes like a bell. "Daddy!" she shouts. He opens his arms wide and lifts her up to his face. Alejandro has grown a bit. He's thicker around the middle and his face is rounded out. She tugs on his moustache and yanks at his goatee. He laughs and holds her tightly in his grip. The feeling of her innocence against his callused body does things to him, makes him feel right. Bernadette reminds him of the custody hearing.

"Next week," she says.

He ignores her.

"Better be there," she presses.

He pulls Jelly against his chest and gives Berni a look that says go fuck yourself. Jelly tilts her head and leans into the nape of his neck.

"Alejandro," she calls out as he walks to the car ignoring her.

4

All day a gang of piranhas have been gnawing at his guts. Tomorrow it will come down to one thing: whether or not he will continue to have rights to see Jelly. He decides that after work he'll hit the bar. When the time comes he showers, slicks his wavy hair back, dashes on a glob of Old Spice, then drives to Intimo where he finds the usual bunch. A few ears hear him out, but before long the only ones left are he and Gigi, the bartender with a sagging face and body like a sack of radishes. He looks at her and decides to keep to himself. Seven shots later he stumbles out.

5

"Fuck you, Bernadette!" Alejandro slurs, punching the steering wheel until his knuckles whiten. "She's my girl too!"

He turns the key and throws the gear into drive, and flies off toward Bernadette's place. He pulls into the alleyway behind her house and kills the engine. He jumps the fence and pounds his fist on the glass door.

"Berni!" he shouts. "Bernadette, get your ass out here!"

A light turns on from inside. Bernadette sees him.

"What the fuck," she says. "You're drunk. Get outta here before I call the cops."

But Alejandro isn't having it. She notices the mad-dog hunger in his eyes and runs to get Jelly and head out the front door. He strangles the back-door handle and it opens. Before Bernadette knows what's happening, he's yanked Jelly from her grip and shoved her out the front door—click!

6

It's 1:47 a.m. and a voice is blaring from a bullhorn, waking up every neighbor and sending the dogs into a yowling hysteria.

"Alejandro, let the baby out," the bullhorn says.

"Fuck you!" he shouts back.

And then a long silence. In her half-sleep, Jelly mutters something.

"I'm right here, mijita. Daddy's here, just sleep," he tells her.

He moves her to the couch and covers her head with a cartoon blanket. He peers between the curtains. A gun is propped behind every bush and parked car. Rifles are aimed and cocked.

"Release Jelly," the bullhorn blasts.

Alejandro says nothing. He stares at photos on the wall. Notices the one where his image is cut out and only Bernadette and the baby remain. The bullhorn squawks again. This time he opens the curtains just enough to stick his hand through and flash a middle finger.

"Alejandro, don't do anything stupid," it calls out.

And again he flips them off. This time with both hands. Every time they call for him to release the baby, he responds by opening up the curtains and exposing a bit more of himself.

7

It comes through the window like a ray of light. The last thing he sees upon falling to the floor are Jelly's little eyes waking up to watch him fall.

8

Everywhere there are frequencies of satellite waves rippling out into the questionable night. Words and sounds and translucent images of siren lights and helicopter beams and white sheets and blank faces reporting live from distant scenarios, all rise up in a flotilla, defying earth's gravity into a single streamlined thread, building up to a flurry of mixed signals and words. And at the end of that thread, Alejandro. Poised in the television box of another man's living room.

The Killer

The man puts the artificial vagina back into its carrying case.
He takes whatever sperm was collected and slips it into a small
cryogenic container and seals it in a box. Because there has been
a string of thefts in Catela, he will make the delivery himself. On
his way home he stops by the post office and sends it express.

It kills him to know that in the last three months over thirty
gallons of bull batter has been stolen and no one's been caught.
Last Monday, after putting in extra hours, the man was walking
home past dark and saw two Mexicans in a pickup truck eyeing
the cattle suspiciously. The man stood there, defiant, waiting to
see if the assholes dared come around again but they didn't.

"What the fuck is this world coming to when a man steals the
sperm right outta the bull," he once told another field hand. "If I
ever catch the sick fucks, God help me, I'll hogtie the bastards
myself."

But not tonight. Tonight, the man plans on erasing the work
week from his mind at the Raisin Day Fair.

At home, he peels out of his work slickers and showers off
whatever bits of white film are stuck to his hair and arms. He

pulls a straight razor from the medicine cabinet and sharpens it against an old piece of stone. He tears the razor across his chin and swipes the stubble off on a wet towel. When he's done shaving, he slathers a wad of Happy-Do pomade over his comb and yanks it through his thinning hair. With his fingertips he tweezes out the rigid tufts that have invaded his ears and nostrils.

Through the open bathroom window he can hear the kids next door, dangling on the avocado tree. They're taunting a dog with rocks and shoes, and the damn thing won't stop barking. He wants to tell the kids to fuck off and leave the dog alone, but knows it's no use, tomorrow they'll be back at it. A radio turns up and now they're listening to rap music. The man hears words like *sucka* and *gat* and *ice* rattling from the speakers. He shuts the window and whatever cool breeze sailed through is now gone. He slips his legs into a new pair of second-hand jeans, slaps a light coat on, and starts off toward the park.

On the streets, a pissant line of bodies shuffles along the sidewalks, where cars are parked at odd angles in the gutters. Beneath every busted street lamp, a boy makes out with a girl until a honk or whistle pulls them apart.

The park glows with electric lights strewn over the trees and tents and fences. Children with spinning neon toys zip by, chasing one another toward the kiddie rides. The air smells like cotton candy and bacon-wrapped hot dogs and spilled beer.

Beneath a large tent, a nine-piece Oaxacan banda lights the crowd up. He knows they are from Oaxaca because it says so on the backs of their yellow blazers. Alongside the musicians, four women decked in shimmering dresses dance with pineapples on their heads, and the little girls who sit on their father's shoulders point and laugh at the spectacle. The man stands at the back of the crowd and sips his cider. A woman next to him puffs on a cigarette, and the smoke snakes into his nostrils and burns his eyes so he moves away, closer to the stage.

Up front, he is able to see all the members of the band, and he thinks he recognizes the accordion player. A kid he met at the international ag show last spring. Something of a goddamn bull sperm wiz. The blunt nose and slanted eyes, that thick black crop-top, there's no mistaking him. The kid works over at Hoyt's dairy.

The man knew Jules Hoyt from his early days on the rodeo circuit. They'd competed out in Woodlake for several years, neither of them taking home the Gold Horseshoe Cup, or the Silver Buckle for that matter. He remembers Hoyt being too lanky of a man to stay on for more than a few seconds. Plus, he was so damn tall his boot heels were practically digging trenches.

The man, like most farmers around Catela, didn't consider Jules Hoyt a farmer's farmer. Not because he employed mostly illegals, but because the guy never requested a single piece of paper from his workers. The least he could do was dummy some up. It was obvious Hoyt didn't give a rat's ass who was working for him, plain and simple. He probably had a whole mess of rapists milking his cows or tending his heifers. It didn't matter to him, so long as the money kept coming in. And though the man has never said this to his face, a part of him blamed Hoyt for the stolen sperm.

The man lowers his hat over his eyes and watches as the kid's thin fingers bounce over the white buttons of the accordion. He sees how the girls are crazy for him. The way they scream when he hits a solo, or when he tucks his chin down and spins a full circle. He doesn't understand what they see in him, or in the music for that matter. It sounds like a car wreck, he says to an onlooker. But the onlooker ignores the man and moves a few steps closer to the stage.

Later that night he's at the band shell.

"Can you hear . . . ?" a petite girl says in a low voice, as she taps the microphone. "Is this thing on?"

Someone howls from the audience, "Nam Fon! Go girl!" And then several more voices light up and call her name. The girl lowers her eyes and giggles.

The man looks over the heads of the audience and then back at the girl.

"I just wanna thank my sister May . . . and my little sister Bee. They helped me to sell all the tickets."

Screams spill from the ferris wheel and then fade off.

"I thought I could only sell twenty, maybe fifty. But I never thought I would sell one hundred and eighty seven tickets. I don't know. Thank you."

The people clap and the Raisin Day Queen, along with the other girls, steps off the stage. A fat woman holding a pickled pig's foot shouts out, "That's okay, mija, you still my reina!" One of the girls on stage smiles and acknowledges with a wave. The woman shouts again and the man watches her entire body jiggle. Even the loose tendons on the pig's foot jump like they're made of rubber.

He wanders from booth to booth, eyeing the junk food, and the dart games and cheap plastic toys. Near the Gravitron he watches a tired mother shovel spoonfuls of funnel cake into her daughter's mouth. Over at the fast pitch he sees a father trying to impress his son by chucking baseballs sloppily against a fence. He spots a kid toting a dog leash with an invisible dog at the end, and this sparks a memory.

Back when the man was a child and his family pulled potatoes in Fort Lupton, Colorado, they had lived in El Campo del los Tejanos, a migrant worker trailer park. On one especially humid night, they heard a baby crying. It cried for hours and wouldn't let up. None of the families in the camp had any babies. Most of the children were already in middle school like him.

The first few nights passed with the same baby crying at the same hour. By the end of the week the neighbors got to talking. They wondered whose baby it was, and what unholy thing they were doing to it that it cried so damn much. A few of them rallied together one Sunday afternoon and knocked on every door in the trailer park. All had heard the baby crying too, and had been wondering the same thing. It went on like this for another week. Until one night, fed up with losing sleep, his old man decided to stay up for as long as it took to track down the cry.

He was sitting on his couch, dozing off, when it started up. He looked out the window, but saw no lights on in any of the trailers. He opened his front door and stepped out into the night. The cry grew louder still. The man ran back inside the trailer and pulled his hunting rifle from beneath his bed and loaded it.

"Whatchoo gonna do with that?" his wife asked.

"I'll show 'em I ain't playin' is what am gonna do. Maybe if I fire off a round the noise'll shut that baby up."

"You gonna wake everybody up with that thing."

"I ain't fit to argue 'bout this," he replied, cocking the gun and heading out.

When he got to the front door, again he heard the crying, but now it appeared to come from behind him. He turned around quickly and listened for it, but it stopped. And then it started back up. It was coming from the kitchen. He aimed his rifle at the refrigerator. It stopped again, this time for good.

He went and sat down on the couch, placed the rifle on his lap, and dozed off.

An hour later, he awoke to a blue ghostly image hovering in the kitchen. She was toting a dog on an invisible leash. Both stood staring at the man. He jumped from the couch and aimed his rifle at her and fired. The round blew a hole through the refrigerator and lodged itself into the wall.

The next morning the man and his son pulled the refrigerator from its place against the wall. After they emptied it of food, they lugged it outside and hauled it to the dump yard.

An hour later they returned to the trailer and began repairing the hole. The boy was given a pickax and was told to start tearing the flimsy wall apart. Meanwhile, his father sorted out the electrical wires that were destroyed by the blast, and began taping them back together.

The boy hammered away at the sheets of particleboard and stucco, tearing off piece by piece with the pickax. He began to see that some of the slabs were stained a deep purple. He continued to pull at the wall and found more and more pieces with the same discolorations. In some places, the color was caked on thick, in black and red blotches. When the father saw this, he began to tear the wall apart. He found the inside of the walls slaked in red. One of the pieces had a garment clinging to it. It was drenched in black. The man peeled the garment off and saw that it was a small Mexican-style blanket.

"What is it Poppa?" the boy asked, but the man didn't answer.

He watched as his father began pulling baby clothes, bibs, and tiny socks out of the wall. A blanket with the name Hortencia embroidered on it. Bonnets and little shoes, everything doused or flecked with black. His father shouting out, "Animals!"

The man decides to call it a night. He walks past the beer garden and sees that the borrachos have begun sizing each other up, talking trash and staggering about. Meanwhile, the blue suits are circling them like vultures, just waiting for a slip-up. He spots the Raisin Day Queen over by the bathrooms. The crown shines on her head like a star in the dense night. She's with a bald guy who's got one hand on her ass while he's feeling her up with the other. The man watches them stick their tongues down each other's throats for a good five minutes, until they come up for air. When they're done, the queen readjusts her crown and fixes her bra straps, and then kisses the dude goodnight.

The man starts home. He cuts across a small bridge and walks along the embankment. Slowly his eyes adjust to the night, and he can see the black gnarled shapes of harvested plum trees, row after row. He thinks about how six months ago this same picture would have looked entirely different. There would have been splashes of color everywhere, stretched out for miles across Catela. But now, from this angle, at this time of night, the way the wiry trees stand in crippled formation looks like something out of a toxic nightmare.

He walks for twenty minutes, until he comes to an oak tree and has to stop to shield a cloud of dust from his eyes. When it clears he can see Hoyt's place in the far-off distance. The man continues walking, and his eyes scan over the loose shadows and unusual shapes sprawled out over the landscape. He glances over to where the cattle are gathered, and catches what looks like a person scurrying around the perimeters of the farm. The man comes to another oak tree and positions himself in its shadow for a better look.

A short figure emerges from behind a plow and picks up what looks like a box, and then begins staggering toward the dirt road in a hurry. The man jumps to the other side of the canal and runs ahead. He keeps his eyes on the stranger as the stranger leaps over the narrow rows of irrigation cradling his box. I see you, you son-of-a-bitch, the man says to himself, and takes off running up the dirt road. He sees the stranger quickly approaching, and knows he's headed for the bridge near the large irrigation pumps, so the man hurries to beat him there.

The pumps churn and the sound of water splashing won't let the man hear when the stranger is approaching, so he slips between the shadows of the pump and waits until he can see him. He spots a loose pipe on the ground and picks it up. The man tries making out the shape and size of the box. If he could only hear over the noise, he'd listen for the clang of jars or other small containers capable of keeping bull sperm. He sees the stranger stop and set his box down carefully on the ground. The stranger looks around and then unzips his pants and pisses into the canal. The man grips the pipe and can feel his heart racing. The stranger lights up a cigarette and stays put. The man leans out of the shadow for a better look at the box. In what little light the moon lets off, he sees there is something shiny about it. The containers, he thinks to himself. He pulls his head back and waits. The stranger begins to sing something in Spanish. The man shakes his head, and then runs his fingers through his hair and takes a deep breath. He looks across the landscape and sees the cattle standing still as statues. He wonders who the hell is stupid enough to steal bull sperm in the first place. It's not like there's a pawnshop on every corner quick to offer cash for the stuff. And unless it's stored properly and you know what you're doing, you only got three maybe four days of shelf life on it.

The stranger finishes his smoke, and then stops singing to pick up the box. The man watches him reach down and lift it up gently with both hands and then cradle it. He grips the pipe tighter still, and then holds his breath as the thief staggers past the pumps and begins to sing again. The man lifts the pipe above his head and when the thief's back is to him he brings the pipe down over his soft skull. The thief lets out a cry and then falls face down in the dirt. The box tumbles into the canal.

"I caught you, you son-of-a-bitch," the man says, spitting on the guy and kicking dirt at him. "Thought you'd get away with this, you waste. You goddamn filth."

A string of fluid leaks from the thief's hair onto the dirt, but the man can see his shoulders rising and falling, and he knows he is still alive. When the body finally stops shaking, the thief mumbles something.

"What's that you saying, son-of-a-bitch? Speak up." He kicks the thief in the ribs, and then squats down to roll him onto his back. He sets the pipe on the ground and grips his shoulders and heaves him over. It's Jules Hoyt's boy. The Oaxacan kid.

The man runs to fetch the box from the canal, and when he pulls it from the water he discovers that it's an accordion.

"Aw, fuck me," he cries. The kid's eyes roll back in his head. "Goddammit!" He paces in a circle and then stands over the boy and stares down into his eyes. "Get up," he says, and then he leans over and slaps the kid's face and the kid's eyes go white. "Aw shit. Fuck me."

The man grabs the pipe and flings it into the canal. "Get up," he screams. "Get up I said." The man grabs the kid from the shoulders and tries lifting him to his feet but the body drops like a log. The man pounds his fist into his temple and doesn't know what to do. He feels a surge rise in his chest and his throat closes. "Aw, fuck me!" he screams. "Get up you bastard!" He kicks the kid's legs and then collapses on his body. "Get up, get up," he says, pounding his fists into the kid's chest. "I'm telling you to get up, goddammit!" He punches the kid in the throat, and then the face, and the kid's mouth opens and he gasps for air. "Ho shit, take them motherfuckin' breaths!" He smashes the kid's face with his knuckles and spits at him, and the kid grovels and gasps for air, but the man weeps and slaps the kid for making him weep. "This is your fault!" he screams. "Your goddamn fault!"

The kid's muddy tongue juts from his mouth like a sword and his eyes open and the pupils stare right at the man and the man steps back and screams. "Don't you dare, you fuck! Don't you dare look at me." Incoherent words gurgle from the kid's mouth, and the man snorts, and then pulls his buck-knife from his pocket and opens it. He looks around and then leans down and grabs the kid's tongue and cuts it right out of his mouth. "You ain't gonna rat me out, you fuck." The kid's eyes are fixed on the man, and the man sees this, and another thought comes to him and he grabs the accordion and smashes it down onto the kid's accusing glare.

When all is done the killer sits with the kid. When he notices the pearl sky of morning glowing over the Sierra Nevadas, he reaches for the accordion. He pulls its straps over one shoulder and then heaves the kid's body over the other. He walks like this, for several minutes, until he can no longer carry the boy. He dumps the body into the canal, but the water isn't deep enough to hide it, so the man covers it with fallen oak tree branches, grass, rocks, until the body blends into the landscape.

He hurries home, before there are no more shadows to hide beneath, before Catela wakes up to the weekend. He trashes the accordion in a dumpster near his house. But then he fears someone will find it there, so he digs it back out and takes it home with him.

It's five-thirty in the morning when he walks through his front door. He grabs a plastic trash bag from beneath the sink and places the accordion inside it. He strips naked and puts his clothes in the bag too. He ties the bag and leaves it sitting in the kitchen, next to the refrigerator. Then he grabs the remote control and walks over to the couch and lays down on it. He turns the television on to *Good Day News*, pulls a blanket up over his cold naked body, and waits.

Querida Catela

There is a bullet hole in my fence that stares at me every time I walk up the driveway. A hole, where every year around Thanksgiving a family gathers and brings flowers and candles and sits around and talks until the pigeons fade into darkness. I'm left to watch those flowers dry up and flake off. Left to dream about that hole, time and again, the same dream. Sometimes, I fall into the hole and can't get my footing. Other times, my right eye *is* the

hole, looking out over the front yard, and my body is the fence post, and I feel as if I've seen more than I care to.

Querida Catela, I hate the gunk collection strewn across your streets, of paper cups and chip scraps. Hate the way your pigeons nest atop swamp coolers and neon signs, and scratch out the faces of crumbling statues and dead cars, as if they have nothing better to do but sit around and gossip. I hate the sound of your pickup trucks that gag and lurch, and the stink of cow shit that permeates the pores and taints whatever hint of beauty that may have once had a chance. I hate the way your dogs bark. I hate your greasy streets stained with the hot juices of drooling fruit trucks and roadkill left to stew in the sun. I hate how the winos push baby strollers filled with meaningless shit like a broken plate, or ax handles, or stickers of old cartoons. I hate that when I am standing in line at the grocery store there is always some braless grandmother with gargantuan titties and a mole on her neck, bad-mouthing her young grandson, whose eyes hint of escape.

Catela, when I see you like that, standing there with your mouth wide open, it's as if you are staring at me dead in the eye, like I am nothing more than a germ writhing beneath a lens, where on the other end is a mind that I cannot for the life of me come to terms with.

Last night I dreamt that I had escaped you, and was living among the lush green of some mountain paradise, like Vermont or Col-

orado. I dreamed I was older. Much older. And that I had a family—a wife and two girls, and that we sat on the rim of a wide
meadow and were watching a herd of elk. It was bugling season
and the leaves were turning from blue to red, and wherever there
were luminescent washes of gold I could see the sun inside the
mountain. And within that sun there was everything.

We finished watching the elk hump one another, and then
rode our little car home to our place beside a creek. That night it
began to snow, and my wife who had never seen snow before, ran
out into the night with her arms spread wide open. And when she
had embraced the falling fluffs of white long enough, she tilted
her head back and opened her mouth, right before that pristine
whiteness erased her entirely.

> Sincerely,
> Tlaloc

Days of Fertility

Concerning the grito of the unborn

The building is located on the outskirts of Catela, near Sun Citrus Packing plant, where out front all the ex-cons and recovering junkies hover, chain smoking, waiting for their cheese and morphine omelets to kick in. Years ago the whole scene would've looked entirely different. Instead of this bunch, you would have found paisas and harvest gypsies and other windblown fruit gathered around the gates, waiting for work.

The room itself reminds me of a principal's office. A small gray-washed square with flyers hanging at odd angles and mini-blinds shut over the only two windows. There is a pile of magazine covers but the magazines themselves are missing. The covers are just tissue-soft skins, barely intact as they get passed on from one hand to another.

"Ya know the only difference from them and *us*," I hear one girl say while pointing at a cover, "is that they got all the money they need to make their problems go away."

"Tell me about it," friend replies, sucking the acrylic off her thumbnail.

Talina has been working at Pato's Carniceria for almost a year

now. For five bucks an hour, she cleans out the carcasses in the
back room with a hose that hardly has any power. Cows, goats,
pigs, chickens, you name it, she cleans it. They bring the animal
in skinned, gutted, and life-warm, and she sticks the hose down
their throats and pulls it through the chest tunnel and out the asshole and back again. She buries her two thin fingers into the eye
sockets and shovels that gelatinous meat out, careful not to pop
one because the old Portuguese men pay good money for eyeball,
and then she rams the hose down there too. She can't stand the
brains. The venous white noodles that she's forced to scoop out
with a spatula and place into Ziploc baggies. She thinks that if she
is ever going to catch some deathly disease, it's going to come
from the brains. "If you ain't gonna insure me," she tells Pato,
"then at least I should have benefits." She demands benefits. He
agrees, and offers as a benefit a free choice-cut of meat on Fridays. Good Fridays.

Talina don't want a baby. She's told me this many times. Said
she *used to* want one, way back before her ex was an hijo de puta.
Back when she was sure her uterus was still whole.

"I'm not so convinced anymore," she said. "Not after all the
shit I've done to my body. Fuck, not after the hijo de puta
pounded it to mush."

"It ain't mush," I would say to her. "At least it don't feel like
that to me."

She would smile and run her hand over my forehead. "Sometimes you're way too sweet for your own good."

When she told me about it, she was plain-faced and cool as
hell. No guilt trips or funny movidas, just straight out with it.

"Look Tlaloc, I'm pregnant, alright. I don't want you getting all
stupid on me, I mean we got something cool, you know. I don't

expect shit from you and you don't expect nothing from me and that's cool."

"You think it's my baby?"

"Of course it's you. You're the only one I been with for awhile. I'm not proud of that, but shit, it ain't like I got dudes knocking down my door to get with me. Yeah, I'm sure it's you."

"What about that time you said you hooked up with your ex again? At Intimo's, remember that? You said you got smashed and did something stupid that night."

"Fuck Tlaloc, that was like three months ago. I know you don't know shit about making babies, but this only happened about six weeks ago, if that. And I ain't been with no one since."

"How do you know for sure?"

"Cuz I'm late—way late."

"And you've never been late before?"

Talina reached into her bra and pulled out a cigarette and lit it. She stood there quietly, over her kitchen sink. "Look," she said, blowing a sloppy smoke halo into the air, "I told you, you ain't got nothing to worry about, alright? You're off the hook, I swear it. I ain't like all those little girls you're used to dating, mijo. I mean, I ain't gonna try pulling some shit on you, alright? I'm serious. Serious as cancer."

I tried to get a good read on her, but she turned her back to me, then smashed out her cigarette and started washing dishes. After standing there a few minutes without a comeback, I walked up to her from behind and wrapped both hands around her waist and pushed up against her. She leaned her head back against my chest and I kissed her neck until her skin pimpled. I kissed the spot behind her ear, near her hairline, and she shut her eyes and backed up into me. I yanked her shorts down and stuck my hand up her shirt and right there on the floor beneath the sink we did it hard and quick, sloshing around beneath the leaky pipes. And when I unloaded I just went for it, right in her, didn't think twice. The damage was already done.

I look at the clock that hangs on the wall. It's been over an hour since she walked behind those doors. I go over to the desk clerk.

"How long before she comes out?"

The clerk fixes her glasses and stares up at me. "It takes about six hours."

"Six hours?"

She nods. "We keep her in observation after the procedure for a couple of hours before we can let her leave. It's just a precaution," she says.

I look around the lobby and then return to my seat. I'm the only guy in the room, and I feel like all these knocked-up chicks are giving me mal de ojo. Like I'm the one who popped their little dream bubbles and sent their whole world spinning into oblivion. The chatter in my head kicks up and I can almost hear the hexes being concocted in the backs of their minds. I consider leaving, but am stuck between feeling like an asshole and reassuring myself that Talina doesn't need me here anyway. Not now at least. Not for another six hours. When the clerk walks away from her desk I make my move.

Outside, the day is hot and overcast. I stroll out onto the dirt road near the parking lot. A frail-looking woman in a wheelchair is posted up near the back end of a pickup truck. Her hair is white and balding. When I pass her she pushes her arm out at me and is holding a white coffee can with a cross painted on the side of it. Her head hangs over her left shoulder and she stares up at me from the corner of her eye. She doesn't mumble a word to me. Her eyes do all the saying. Her hand shakes and the can dances in her fingers, and I pretend to look elsewhere and move on before she hits me up for change. I move out past the parked cars, and continue walking toward the edge of a nearby fallow plum field. In the distance, the uprooted trees are piled into monstrous stacks, and there's at least a hundred of these piles spanning out onto the horizon and the land looks like some Armageddon panorama. I find a soft spot in the dirt and sit and wonder how this'll change things between Talina and me.

I had been writing more frequently now. Not just the same old journal scribble, but actual poems. Last summer I read a few pieces to Talina and she liked them. Then she asked if I would write her a piece about the seasons.

"It'll take awhile," I said, "that kind of thing takes time."

"That's fine," she replied, "maybe you could have them for our anniversary?"

"Since when do you and I have an anniversary?"

"Fuck you, I'm just saying, from the time we met, you know."

Since it was the end of summer already, I figured I'd start with autumn. When the time came, I watched the tule fog roll in, and looked hard for the words to describe how in each single leaf I saw a piece of sunlight in it. I'd walk down the alleyway behind the carniceria, where trees hung over fences and leaves blanketed the broken asphalt and gaping potholes, and I'd lift up a leaf, several of them, and smell them, and roll them over my face, and sometimes I'd bite into them.

And then by winter everything froze, and I mostly stayed indoors, observing from the kitchen window all the gray that ate up Catela. Only once in awhile I'd go outside, just to take in a deep breath and feel the sting of air enter my lungs like daggers.

As for spring, that was just too easy.

And now it's summer again, but this time the poem doesn't come so quick. Besides, I'm in no mood to be writing some romantic shit, not now. For the next few hours I sit there sweating out the heat, jotting down lines in my notepad.

When Talina comes out from behind the doors, she's got one hand on her purse and the other gripping a cigarette. She stops to light it up and then pulls her shades out and plops them on her face and walks toward me. I got both hands in my pockets and my guts are tying themselves up. She stops at my shadow and offers me a drag. I take it and inhale and consider whether or not it would be stupid to ask how it went.

"You still here, huh?" She says.

I lower my head and exhale the smoke.

"Figured you'd be long gone by now."

I don't know what to say, so instead I take another drag and hold onto it.

"It's done," she says, reaching her hand out for the smoke.

I pass it to her and release. "Oh," I say.

She takes a last drag and drops the cigarette on the dirt and squashes it with the toe of her shoe. She pulls out her lipstick and begins to line her upper lip and then her bottom one perfectly, without a mirror. I take a few steps back to give her some privacy. I wipe the sweat from my neck with my shirt collar.

"What now?" I say.

"I need the cash," she replies.

I look at her, and decide to keep my mouth shut. She stops with the makeup and stares at me. I dig into my pocket and pull out a single crisp Benjamin Franklin.

"There it is." I slap it down in her hand.

"I gotta get back to work," she says, tucking the bill into her purse. She hesitates. "Look Tlaloc . . . Pato can't know about this shit, alright? Believe it or not, his fat ass is Catholic."

"This the same dude who's always got his hands on you?"

"I know, huh. Ain't that some shit?"

I spit on the ground and put both hands back into my pockets. Talina starts to walk off, and she's about five feet ahead of me now, and I can't tell if she wants me to follow her, or if I should just go my own way. She takes a few more steps and looks over her shoulder. I honestly don't give a damn either way. She gets on my nerves sometimes. Most times. Now.

"You coming?" she says.

I wait a little, so as not to look like some lost perro chasing after the first hand that lowers itself. She turns around and begins to walk away. Black clouds roil in the distance. Her body shrinks into the landscape, but she keeps on, slipping away. The air smells like dead skunk. Like wet earth. Like Talina's skin on a better day.

Four

Del dicho al hecho hay mucho trecho.
It's a long distance between saying and doing.

LATIN PROVERB

The Eleventh Step

2000

Concerning the escape

Downtown Los Angeles is wired like a pubis of nervous spiders. Besides the smog of the gagging industrial machine gone awry, a clot of traffic extends from the San Fernando Valley down between the dusty toes of Riverside. Everything—from fences to high-rise buildings to palm trees and fire hydrants—is tagged. The sky is sickly, and the clouds hang like jowls. The people who populate the streets mad-dog their own reflection, and the rhythm is like something out of the robotic eighties. Stamp and move. Beat over beat. When the sun is out, the air is sticky hot and smells like piss. At night, it cools to coat level.

I don't know what I'm doing here. I mean, I know what I'm doing here, but I don't know if it's really happening, or if I'm making this up, and really I am passed out stoned in the grape field behind my house. Here is what I do know. There is a round-trip bus ticket in my wallet, along with three moist dollar bills. I have a backpack full of poems, and I am expected to read one in a café at Olvera Plaza. Eight hours of bus ride down the dogleg of Highway 99, for one poem. If I'm lucky, I'll get two. But I'll settle for one. The reading begins at nine o'clock, and right now it's seven-thirty, and I don't know a single soul in this city, much less how to get around. I start at the ticket counter.

"Excuse me, how do I get to Olvera Plaza from here?"

The woman looks up at me. "Come again?"

"Olvera—is it nearby?"

She snaps the gum in her mouth and nods. "Just aks a cab, they'll take you."

I look out the large windows that face the back part of the station. Cabbies are hovering like vultures, pecking at stragglers.

"How far is it?" I ask the woman.

She looks me in the eye. "'Bout four miles from here."

"All I got is three bucks," I tell her.

"Ain't my problem."

I look outside again and notice the sky bruising. "Can I walk it from here?"

"Not unless you lookin' to get jacked." She snaps her gum, and shakes her head. "You don't wanna be caught on Eleventh Street at night. Not by youself. Hell, not even wit your crew."

I look around at all the worn faces that fill up the lobby. Mostly there are people with endless bags of shit, and crying babies and darting eyeballs. People who look worse off than me. I turn back to the woman. "Can you just tell me how to get there?"

"Franky," she calls out. A muscular homeboy walks out from behind a stack of boxes. "Franky, explain to this man why he shouldn't be tryin' to roll up Eleventh by hisself. He thinks I'm playin'."

Franky looks me up and down. "You best listen to this

woman," he says. "You don't want to be out there, homie, especially not looking like you do."

The woman laughs. Franky is at least two hundred pounds
bigger than me, so I let it slide. "I ain't trying to clown you," he
says, "I'm just sayin' it's obvious you ain't from here." The woman
nods. Franky looks me in the eye and walks off.

"Don't take it personal. Hell, I won't even go down that street
myself," the woman says.

I spin my head around and check out the lobby. I don't know
what I'm looking for exactly. An opportunity, maybe. Some little
bit of nothing I can turn into something. But it's all the same people with the same numb faces. The woman notices my despera-
tion. She pulls a piece of paper from her drawer and clicks a pen.

"Shit," she says, drawing a straight line. "Look, you wanna stay
on Eleventh, 'bout three or four miles. You fast?" I nod. "Good.
Should take you less than an hour if you fast."

I grab the paper off the counter and head out.

She yells behind me, "I best not see yo' ass in the news tonight
neither. Talkin' 'bout some dead kid from who knows where got
jacked."

Outside, the cabbies are busy slouching against the bumpers
of their cars and talking on cell phones. One looks at me and
opens his door. I pass him up. On the other side of the street a
couple of trucks with camper shells sit idled. They look like every
other truck in Catela. Behind the wheel sits some fat coyote with
cheap sunglasses and a cigarette hanging from his mouth. I can
tell they're coyotes by the way they stare. Like you're some fresh-
off-the-boat wetback who ain't got a prayer in Los Estados without
their help. Seeing them made me think of the three guys that got
busted back in Bakersfield.

It happened on the 99 just outside Delano. The bus pulled to the shoulder and dust floated up around us. When it settled, there on the road were two green Suburban trucks. The bus driver stood up from his seat and took his hat off. He looked back and shifted his eyes over the seats carefully.

"Everyone stay put," he said. "This'll all be over quick, and we'll get moving again."

He opened the door and stepped out into the glaring sun. From my window I could see him, talking to the officers. Of the four uniforms, three were Chicano. One was white. The bus driver motioned with his hands. He lifted up three fingers and pointed to the back end of the bus. They consulted with one another, and then nodded their heads.

A nervous chatter erupted in the bus. People whispered and gripped their handbags and looked around. Those who had children pulled them closer, ordering them to behave themselves and play with their muñecas quietly. The old woman seated across from me reached into her purse and pulled out her escapulario, threading it between her fingers.

Behind me bodies were rustling. Two men scurried into the bathroom and locked the door. One slithered beneath the seats. His boot poked out into the aisle. A woman whispered to him and he drew it in.

Two of the officers circled the outside of the bus while the other two boarded. The white one addressed us in gringo-Spanish. "Nessy tamos ver su micas. Poor favor zacanlos."

Half the passengers opened their wallets and pulled out their cards. Others sat still and remained silent, including me. The offi-

cers walked slowly and examined every card that was held up. The
rest of us were asked one simple question.

When they reached the back of the bus, heads turned and
breaths were held. The officer knocked on the door. It was quiet.
He tried again. Noises came from inside.

"Sálganse," he ordered. The noises stopped and he tried again.
"Sálganse!"

The latch clicked and two men stumbled out, smiling like
third graders caught in a game of hide-n-seek. The officer took
them to the truck and then returned. The guy snaking beneath the
seats had grown restless. One of his arms poked out into the aisle
and the officer dragged him out from underneath. He squirmed
for a second, but quickly gave up. He joined the other two, and a
few minutes later off they drove. And just like that, we were back
on the road.

The sun is in the ocean now, and two dim stars flirt in the distance. It's five past eight. I put my bag down, sit on a bench, and
consider waiting for a miracle. The silhouettes of buildings look
like black Legos stacked and wrapped with miles of telephone
wire. Buses bully in and out. A car slithers from an alleyway and
bangs over a pothole before hissing back into darkness.

The mind has a funny way of messing with you when you least
expect it. Years ago, I read the biography of the Night Stalker. But
only now do I remember that the downtown L.A. Greyhound station was where he targeted his marks. This station. Back when he
was just a shady tecato looking for a fix, he'd vulture the parking
lot and lobby and bathrooms, scoping out the deadbeats and pendejos who walked around with their heads in the heavens. In his

early days, he was mugging to keep the demons of habit fed. But then later, once his skill was honed to the tee, he would pluck heads randomly from this station and not think twice about it.

I pick up my bag and cross the street to McDonald's. The light from the golden arches sign snaps and illuminates only a small section of the street, the rest of it is blacker than pitch. I pull the last three bills from my pocket and go inside and buy the fattest cup of coffee they have on the menu. It's the only weapon I can think of. I look at my watch and see that it's eight-twenty now. I have forty minutes left, and only seventy-two cents to my name. I walk back outside and stare down the long narrow strip of darkness that is Eleventh Street. The only speck of light comes from a needle-point, right in the center of the abyss, but it's a trillion light-years away. Everything else falls into a hole, which according to the woman at the bus station is at least three miles wide. I shift my eyes to find the needle-point in the darkness, just to be sure. I see it clearly now, flickering like a beacon. It's coming from the Plaza.

The first ten steps are the easiest. You're still close enough to change your mind. I stop at the tenth step and look over my shoulder. I can still hear voices coming from the bus station, and see people dragging themselves in and out of the building. Maybe the eleventh step isn't so bad, I think to myself. But then I look up that long dizzying stretch of asphalt, and hesitate. Shit, it's going to be harder than I thought. I look again. You've got to be a crazy motherfucker to take the eleventh step, I say to myself. You've got to be crazy or high or some type of shape-shifter to even think about taking the eleventh step, my mind replies. Yet there I go taking number eleven like it's nobody's business. And then the twelfth, and thirteenth come along, and so do fourteen and fifteen. Now twenty, twenty's a motherfucker too. It could be that twenty is the real eleventh. I stop at nineteen and look back, and now I can no longer hear the voices as clear as I did. I take a drink of my coffee and look for the needle-point. I see it, but it's exactly the same size as it was nineteen steps ago. I drink more coffee, and then toss the cup half-full into the gutter. I tighten the straps on my backpack and take off running up the street, high knees, hauling ass for as long as my legs will carry me.

Fifteen minutes later, I stop to catch my breath and look back again. This time the McDonald's sign glows in the far-off distance, and I can't see any part of the bus station. Sweat slides down my cheeks and forehead and I wipe it off and move on. But I'm quiet now. As quiet as my feet and breathing will allow me to be. I hear rustling in the alleyways. Abandoned building after abandoned building, strange little movements spew from cracks and shadows. Shreds of paper dance with invisible gusts of wind that stir up old urine and decaying rats. I keep my eyes scanning left to right. I'm in the gut of L.A.'s Bermuda Triangle and there's no telling what the hell is lurking.

I see headlights cruising toward me, but then I don't see them, and then they reappear again. I consider ducking behind a garbage bin, but then the car vanishes for good. I run some more. Time is passing quick. I run until my back is drenched. Until I can feel my heart beating through my jugular. And then I keep running. And then I stop again, only to breathe. And then I start right back up. Running, until it starts to feel good, in my legs and chest and arms, and for a second I go zigzagging down the middle of the street, pushing myself to keep going. The needle-point thickens and I'm at full tilt now, arms swinging, chest heaving, legs pumping. I'm cutting through the unknown, and the more I think about it the more I can feel fear trickling in, trying to grab hold of me. So I push harder, away from the bus station. Away from my thoughts. Away from everything familiar. Away.

I think I might be losing my damn mind when I start to smell Chinese food in the air. I run and it grows stronger, stronger still. Until I stop running and start sucking in enormous gulps of breath. And there it is again, Chinese food. I look toward the needle-point and spot a plume of smoke rising above a building. I walk toward the smoke, and toward the needle-point, taking my time, fanning out my shirt in the cool air. Slowly, the thin light begins to blur itself into a single street lamp. And then several street lamps appear. I pass each one, and then restaurants, and traffic. People shuffling in and out of storefronts. I walk toward a bench and throw my body onto it.

Lying down I look up and see a sign that reads, Historic Olvera Plaza. I look at my watch and it's ten minutes past nine. I sit up and check the storefronts for any sign of a café. Everywhere there are restaurants, and boutiques, and musicians prowling gringo tourists.

Across the cobblestone pathway is a small white building. The door is open and a few people are going in. When my shirt and face are mostly dry, I walk over to see if this is the place. From outside, I can hear voices, and chairs shifting, mixing with the sound of spoons against ceramic cups, music playing from a stereo. My stomach turns and it feels like my gut is trying to eat itself. I'm hungry as hell.

I hike my backpack over my shoulder and walk through the door. It's a small room. So small that I take it all in with just one

glance. There are six people here, including me. Everyone seems
to know each other. I walk in and dump my backpack down on
the table and heads turn and stare. I open it and pretend to file
through some poems. A hand taps my shoulder, and I look to find
its owner. Standing above me is a short bald man with no eyebrows or facial hair.

"Tlaloc?" he asks, raising his brow skin.

I nod and put up a smile for the guy. "Darwin?"

He bobs his head. "Glad you made it."

Darwin is Chicano. I know because his shirt says so. I'm also
guessing that he wasn't born with that name. Was probably named
Dario, but as an undergrad came across a copy of *The Descent of
Man*, and decided he'd kick off his own evolution starting with his
birth tag. I shake Darwin's hand and he offers me a cup of coffee
—on the house. I accept.

"Where're the others?" I ask him.

He gets a look on his face. "Others?"

"The writer's group. The one you told me about in your
emails."

"This is it. Everyone's here," he says, rubbing his slick chin.
He walks behind the counter and carefully pours coffee into a
white cup. Meanwhile, I stare at the individual faces, one by one.
An older woman with blonde hair leans toward me.

"I heard about you from Darwin," she says. "Where you from?"

Darwin sets the cup of coffee down in front of me, and I practically guzzle the whole thing in one shot. The woman watches
and it makes me nervous, and some of the coffee leaks out onto
my shirt. She hands me a paper napkin. I'm intentionally avoiding
her million-dollar question by taking my sweet time wiping myself
off. She doesn't blink an eye. I'm relieved when Darwin gets

everyone's attention and kicks off the reading with a poem of his own.

An hour later, everyone has read except me. The last guy ate up nearly forty minutes on the clock and now it's up to me to wake everyone up. For a second, I think Darwin has forgotten about me. But then he calls my name. I quickly scan through my stack of poems searching for the right one. I know exactly what I'm going to read. I find it and pull it from the pile and the paper feels warm.

I stand up and walk to the front of the room slowly. My hands are quaking like a meth addict's, and I'm hoping that by the time I get there the shaking will stop. I turn to face the audience and all ten eyeballs are aimed directly at me. Darwin is standing in the back of the room with his shiny face, smiling. I look at the blond woman. She's got her arms crossed and is nodding at me. I think about her question.

My breath grows shallow and my head spins. I catch myself by shutting my eyes and taking myself back home for a second. The wilted ditch-banks and faces of kids diving in and out of mud holes enter my mind. The crop dusters swooping over, forgotten dogs wandering the back roads of Catela come to me. The train tracks come to me. The fog and sun and drought come to me. The valley comes to me. I stare at the words on the paper I am holding. The first three especially. And I begin to read:

> *When I die*
> *I want great ceremonies*
> *illuminating gray sulk of olive branches and junk piles*
> *where as a child I threw volcanic stones*
> *at abandoned engines, to witness the resonance*

echo against saffron foothills in autumn
and how the swallowtails fled their mud nests
   and swarmed with bats in dusk
where in the shelter of lemon trees we sexed
and discovered pleasurable sins and made promises
      no sentient being could keep—

I want still shots of the merciless streets
     that boot-stomped faggots in honky-tonk alleys
and soft-spoken cowboys who cocked cold triggers to their temple
igniting Fourth of July   I want panoramas of flamenco red
    whirling in an empty room with a dark-skinned
Mexican healer woman
     swooning men with hips like cliffs without end
     I want ballads and nursery rhymes
    and the morning breath of newborns washed over my skin
I want the fields on fire once the last fruit has been plucked
   and the workers have moved onward for the calling crop beyond,
    carry my body to the gnarled plum tree
uprooted by vast trembling monsters where ethanol and torches await
   along the carbon quiet side of dawn
where roosters caw and cluck the landscape
   billowing smoke from weeping smudge stacks
     gather up the loose vines and sweetest raisins
gather jackrabbit and opossum
  summon the gardener and his blue sage blessing
and the long-haired lowriders and pierce-tongued punks
call on the construction workers, tell them to bring their hammers
     and nail guns

there's work to be done

call the prisons and tell them one of their own has flown the bars

let the truckers ride the hammerlane home

I want sacrifices of swine and bull

stark-naked testimonies of hard and holy life

the infant mind bared before the village

expressions of woeful hearts betrayed

innocence dropped in round sloppy sobs

begging cavernous lungfuls of forgiveness

furious anger and fists pummeling hardpan

quaking tantrums to open the earth

I want vows taken to plunge the frightful depths of the unknown

and never cease for fear of the laughable horizon

that goes untouched, a silent cigar that never ends

windhorses thundering valley floor

everyone and everything divine-drunk

stuttering the narrow present!

When I'm done, the sound of all ten hands clap. Darwin nods and smiles. The blonde woman winks, and I know I should feel good about the whole thing except that—one is all I get.

When it's over I sling my backpack on and go to use the rest room. When I return the entire place is cleared out, except for Darwin. His coat is thrown over his shoulder and he has his keys in hand.

"Where'd everyone go?"

"There's another reading, over at Tropico," he says, "in Echo Park." He fiddles with his keys. I lower my eyes and pretend not to give two shits about it.

"Where you off to?" He asks.

"Nowhere."

He starts off toward the door, and I follow.

"How was the trip here?"

I hesitate for a second, wondering if I should tell him the truth or just give him what he's looking for. I go with the latter.

"It was good," I answer. "No big deal."

He locks the door behind us and puts his coat on. "It's chilly out, eh?" He pulls a beanie cap out of his back pocket and slides it down on his head.

"A little," I say.

"What time's your bus leave?"

I look at my watch. It's almost ten forty-five. "Tomorrow. At seven."

"In the morning?"

I nod. "Ticket was cheaper that way."

He looks up at the sky, and then out toward Eleventh Street. "You got a ride to the station?"

"I can walk it."

"You're crazy. You walk down Eleventh and you won't make it out alive, brother," he says, laughing. I laugh too. "I'll give you a ride. It's only a few miles."

Sitting up all night at the bus station, I watch the people come and go. Mostly Mexicanos. A few Chinos, a few blacks, but that's it. I think of Talina, and the look on her face, that stolen look, like long ago someone reached inside that narrow chest of hers and yanked out all the vital organs and sold them for parts. I see that look in a lot of people I know. I wonder if this is what I look like too.

It's twelve minutes past nine a.m. when the bus maxes out at the top of the Grapevine and slithers through the two hills that part ways and unveil the San Joaquin Valley. I look down the long thigh of Highway 99 until it meets the horizon, and I think about all the small towns that rest between these mountains and Catela. In the big sky an umber cloud shaped like a key drags and casts a shadow over us. It hangs heavy above the valley floor, and then slowly separates in all directions, unlocking the land that stretches out for hundreds of miles and vanishes at both ends.

The Bachelor Party

Concerning the return

The two of you haven't seen each other since you moved to
Colorado, five years ago. It is this fact alone that brings you here.
Otherwise, you couldn't care less about Jesus's bachelor party.
Time has changed you both. Where once you might have actually
given a damn about strippers and getting stoned and yukking it up
in a hotel room filled with knuckleheads, now it does nothing for
you. Besides the beer fat that has accumulated around Jesus's
belly, he hasn't changed a bit. Throwing a bachelor party at the
Blossom Motel is evidence of that.

   The Blossom is the cornerstone of Catela's disintegration. The
first tip-off is the sign propped against a cherry tree that reads,
Vacunzy. And then there's the old swimming pool, a graveyard for
blown-out tires and decomposed bird carcasses.

   You find room #9 and let yourself in. A cloud of weed smoke
wrestles you across the threshold and you cough and scan the
room for Jesus, but it's small and packed tight with bodies. A hand
grabs your shoulder and spins you around.

   "Look what the wind blew in." It's Jesus, and he smirks and

gives you a shoulder hug. "Man, you look the same, loco. Haven't changed."

"You too," you say. "Congratulations."

"Can you believe this shit? I'm finally getting hitched, man."

He hands you a beer, and you open it and take a swig. Both his arms are tattooed up to the biceps, but in all that ink you can't make out a single image. Maybe it's like one of those pictures, you think to yourself, where you have to stand a ways back and squint your eyes until a tiger pops out at you. You begin catching up with one another, talking about the last time you hung out, and what happened to who, and how. He tells you about how his father's panaderia went out of business, and that Horacio and Ebenezer both got deported in the whole ordeal.

"Fucking immigration just barges in one day, practically shooting up the place," Jesus tells you through shiny eyes. "Wanting to see green cards and ID's and all that. My dad told them to go to hell, that all his workers were legal. And why don't they go fucking with the farmers, they're the ones with all the illegals, that's the jackpot over there, he tells them. Not some little breadbasket hole in the wall. They should fuck with the dairies, and packing houses, and those motherfuckers. But a panaderia, that's just chicken shit," he says.

"And then what happened?"

"So they take Horacio and Ebenezer . . . man, you shoulda seen poor Ebenezer, old dude was about ready to have a heart attack right there in the dough. I mean he was breathing hard and all that, sweating panocha. Anyway, they take 'em both in the back of their truck, and after my dad tries everything he can to get them out, he finds out they've already been deported. And then the next day Health Inspection shows up, and my dad knows he's

fucked there, so he says the hell with it and gives up the ghost."
Jesus looks over his shoulder and polishes off his beer. He pulls
another one from his front pocket and cracks it open.

"You should see my pops now. He don't look nothing like he
did back then. He's all sucked up and gray."

"What's he doing now?"

"He's working in Nacho's Garage. Fixing tires and shit like
that. He's alright though."

You both stay quiet for a second, and then you raise your can
to his. "For Ebenezer and Horacio," you say, knowing much more
is riding on this one. Jesus takes a drink and then excuses himself
to the bathroom. He looks back.

"Those bitches should be here any minute, Loc, just chill
awhile."

The room is a single bedder with shag carpeting and wool curtains. Besides the weed, it stinks like a combination of ass and
onion. You look around at all the unfamiliar faces, hammering
down cans of beer, and passing blunts. One gets passed to you
and you nod it off, you've already got a contact high.

Among the faces you spot one that you recognize. It's Zeta.
Except for his thick moustache, he still looks the same. Zeta
makes his way towards you and props himself against the wall.

"What's going down Tlaloc? You just get in?"

You nod.

"You look the same," he says. "Just not as scrawny."

You ignore his comment and take another drink of beer.

"'Member when we used to do runs over at the Four Seasons?"

You nod. "Shit was crazy."

"You used to always chicken out at the last minute, 'member

that?" he says. "And fuckin' Jesus would be grabbing shit like chicharrones and candy, and whatever the fuck was in his way to grab, 'member that shit? And when we used to catch trains, man, now that was fucked up, huh? Those were cheap times, bro."

You take a swig of your beer.

"Strippers?"

"What?"

"That's what brought you here, the strippers, right?"

You smirk and take another sip. "Something like that."

"Me too," he says. He tugs at his zipper and polishes off his beer.

Jesus comes out of the bathroom and walks over to the stereo to turn up the music. It's Akwid, and the speakers sound like they're about to collapse. "Those bitches still ain't here," he says out loud. Everyone turns to look at him. "They better not be expecting any tips from me, cuz the only tip they're gonna get is right here," he says, grabbing his crotch and yanking. Everyone busts up laughing. One guy chokes up his beer and it goes flying onto the wall, and then everyone busts up even more.

A kid (who doesn't look a day older than sixteen) goes to the window and opens the curtains, and takes a peek outside. "I think they're here," he says to everyone. The taut sound of his voice confirms your guess.

Jesus walks over and takes a look. "About time," he says, shutting the curtains.

"Are they fine?" asks a fat guy in a tank top. "They better be."

"The fuck do you know about fine bitches, Flaco, you ain't never seen one but in your dreams," Zeta replies. One guy pokes Flaco's fat arm and Flaco brushes him off.

"Nah man, it's cuz one time I was at this party where they had

some strippers, and these bitches was like ghetto like a motherfucker . . ."

"Those are the best kind," another guy cuts in.

"I'm saying, when these bitches pulled them panties down,
that shit looked like a jungle gym."

"The fuck you mean a jungle gym?"

"Monkey bars, motherfucker. All kinds of piercings and hooks
and swing sets down there . . . goddamn slip-n-slides!"

They knock on the door and Jesus opens it with a smirk on his
face. The strippers are standing there dressed in flashy outfits.
Even through the fog of smoke you can smell that perfume.
Coconut. Vanilla maybe.

"You the Wonder Twins?"

They both nod.

"Come in."

They enter and case the room.

"Who's the lucky man?" the redheaded one asks.

"That's me," Jesus replies.

The expression on every guy's face is exactly the same. They
look like a nursery full of panting babies desperate for mama's tit.
You catch a glimpse of yourself in the mirror and realize this
includes you. The last time you remember looking this stupid was
way back, when you first popped your cherry.

You and Concha were only fourteen, and had secretly been
making out since middle school. One afternoon, while her parents
were at work, you both went skinny dipping in the canal behind
her house. It was a little spot hidden with overgrown cattails and
two small persimmon trees. She brought her little sister's blow-up
plastic alligator along for fun, and thank God she did, because
otherwise your ass would've been plucking out espinas for the

next week. Even though you made a valiant effort, the whole thing lasted one minute. The first fifty seconds spent on just getting up the courage to part her legs, and the remaining ten trying to fight back your juices before you could even put it in. When it was over, Concha put her clothes back on, then went and sat on the bank of the canal and buried her feet in the mud and said nothing. But you—you were paralyzed on that alligator, glaze running down your thigh, flashing a grin so wide your teeth hurt.

Roxanne Rockets is the short and thin one with platinum cropped hair and missile titties. The chubbier one, with deep dimples and red locks that sprawl down to her hefty ass, is Georgia Bush. Roxanne gives Jesus a look.

"Who's picking up the tab?" she asks.

He walks over to her, pulls out his wallet, and slaps five twenties down in her hand.

"That right?"

She counts it, then nods at Georgia, and stuffs the wad in her purse.

"Mind if we use the rest room?" Georgia asks.

"Do what you gotta do, ladies."

Both girls squeeze into the rest room and don't come out for a good ten minutes. Meanwhile, the room cooks and everyone is sweating through their shirts. You move to the back, near the window, and crack it open slightly.

Standing next to you is the kid. His baseball cap is cocked over his right eye, and a half-joint clings to his ear. Across the way, Flaco is tugging his shirt down over his stomach, and you can hear him breathing heavy into his beer. Two guys you don't know are sitting on the bed, and a third is propped against the headboard with his legs up. They're passing a bottle of Night Train between themselves. Zeta peeks out the curtains, pulling at his nose the whole time. You begin to take in the little details. The gum wad on the carpet. The water droplets on the mirror. The speed of your own heart beating. You take it all in and it starts to mess with you, like a bad trip. You wonder why you came here in the first place. You seriously consider getting up and walking out, but before you have a chance to make a move the strippers open the door and start tearing up the room, and now everyone is yelling and whistling.

Roxanne is wearing a fake leather dress and high heels, and Georgia comes out in a sequin number that grips her fat rolls. She makes her way to the stereo and turns the music up. When she bends over you see a thin piece of cloth wedged in her ass crack, and a few guys point and call it out. She smiles and stands up and makes her way toward Roxanne. Roxanne guides Jesus down onto a chair and straddles him, and begins to roll her hips to the beat of the music. Everyone roars and fires up, and beers get passed around. You take one. For the road, you tell yourself.

Georgia gets behind Jesus and throws his head back and plops her titties down onto his face and almost smothers him out cold. When she does this a hand reaches out and pinches her ass. She slaps it away. "No touching!" she says. Jesus has his eyes shut and is thrusting his crotch into Roxanne.

"Take it off," Flaco yells, waving his fat fist in the air, and the guys yell right along, and soon it becomes a chant.

"Take it off! Take it off!"

Roxanne gets off Jesus and so does Georgia, and now both climb onto the bed, heels and all, and start dancing with each other.

Zeta shakes up a can of beer and cracks it open on them, and the girls scream, and suds go flying everywhere, including your shirt and hair. They kick their heels at him and he laughs and pounds what's left in the can, and then grabs another. Jesus licks his hand and slaps Roxanne on the ass. "C'mon, gorda," he says, "show us some titties."

She looks him dead in the eye and flashes a nipple. Then two nipples. Georgia follows her lead. Her nipples are huge discs, dark as plums. Flaco sticks his tongue out and wiggles it at her. She lurches back and pulls her skirt up higher, then higher. He pants and so does everyone else. The chanting starts back up, and now both girls are bent over and fiddling their thongs with their fingers.

Jesus yells at them. "Take that shit off, come on!"

Roxanne peels out of her dress and kicks it onto Jesus's face. He dances with it on his head, and then wads it up and throws it back at her and it almost knocks her off the bed. "Fucker!" she says, undoing her bra.

Georgia climbs off the bed and onto Flaco's lap, and this puts a stupid grin on his face. He sets his beer down, and runs both hands over the fat of her hips. She pulls her dress up over her head and her belly falls out. It's webbed with stretch marks and hangs loose over her panties. Guys start laughing and pointing, but Georgia keeps right on. She rips her bra off and uses it to lasso Flaco's wide neck and pull him toward her. She rises up and bobbles his head with her titties and he sticks his tongue out and licks a nipple and she smacks his face again. "What the fuck?" he says.

"I told you already."

He rolls his eyes and continues to grind her.

Meanwhile, Roxanne has the kid laying down on the bed and is squatting directly over his face. Zeta hands the kid a dollar bill and he sticks it in his teeth and Roxanne squats down and picks it up with her ass cheeks. He does it again and again she plucks it.

Another guy throws himself down onto the bed and pushes the kid off. Everyone laughs at the kid and he gets up and grabs a beer and chugs it. Georgia moves to the empty part of the bed and a second line forms, and she begins taking customers.

It goes on like this for what seems like ever. The strippers float around, sweating, performing tricks like circus poodles. Springing from bed to table, dresser to chair. Swiping asses against zippers, navels to noses. The room thumps to fat beats and voices are shouting over one another, screaming mostly, and for a second it feels like the room is levitating. And just when you start to think it might mellow, thongs come off and get slingshot into the mob. One goes flying across the room and lands on the lamp, its moisture sizzling against the hot bulb. The other ends up on the kid's face and he plucks it off and crunches it against his nose and inhales, then chucks it over to Jesus. Jesus does the same and throws it at you. You catch it and throw it back at him, but he's not looking and it sails past. Both girls are clean-shaven and glistening like glass seals. Flaco stands up and the room instantly appears smaller. His entire shirt is drenched in sweat, and he takes the thing off and chucks it on the floor. His dark skin is curdled with pockmarks.

"Put your fucking shirt back on," Jesus yells at him. "No one wants to see those titties."

Flaco ignores him and pulls up the waistband on his pants.

"Wonder Twins!" he yells. "Wonder Twins, baby!"

The mob starts in. "Wonder Twins!"

Georgia swipes a beer from a guy and chugs it and it spills down her body, and Roxanne licks it off, and then both start leaping back and forth like they're caught up in a santería trance, throwing their heads back and their bodies across the room like deflating balloons. Zeta pulls out a dollar bill and before he can even cash it in it's gone. He pulls another out and waves it and again it's gone. Just like that. And now dollar bills are sprouting up everywhere. Guys are waving them and shouting for their attention.

"Over here, gorda!"

"Over here!"

But as fast as they appear they vanish. Almost as if in thin air. One dollar here, a five over there. And then later, tens and twenties too. All of it, gone. Jesus crams his hand down into his pockets and checks to make sure, but they're both empty.

Both strippers spin around and climb over you and cradle their asses into your crotch, but you don't cough up the goods. Roxanne climbs up on the chair and stands with her oyster staring straight at you. You look away, and begin to feel uncomfortable, so you reach into your pocket for some money, anything, but you have none. The oyster smiles and winks at you and then goes flying off the chair and twirls back into Flaco's pillowy chest. He clinches Roxanne with his tits and then releases. Georgia's turn is next. She digs her face between your legs and pretends to bite down. The guys cringe and awe. You grab her face gently and try pushing her away, but she unzips your pants and digs her hand in. You take her wrist and fling it away and she looks at you like you're some mutant motherfucker from another planet. Jesus looks at you too. Zeta looks at you. The kid and Flaco look at you. They all look at you. And in that moment you don't know what to do, so you pull your zipper up and head for the door, slamming it behind you. You expect someone, Jesus maybe, to open the door and call you back in, but it never happens.

From outside the place sounds like a zoo in full riot. A swell of sound and stench and thundering comes from behind the walls. Any minute you're expecting to see a stampede busting out from behind the door. As you walk to your car you wonder how long the party will go on, or if you'll ever see Jesus again. You wonder why you could care less either way. You look back at the room and decide to leave all these questions there in the parking lot of the Blossom. And then you get in your car and drive away. Wondering how long before, or if, anyone will notice you've been missing.

Epilogue

I had no intentions of writing an epilogue. The book is done. The stories should live on as is. But then I turn the television on and see that in the town of Orosi, three separate drive-by shootings happened within the past twenty-four hours. And now there are six people dead. Six separate mothers and siblings grieving. Six young breaths cut short to answer for. And all this in a town of barely one thousand.

Last week, in my neighborhood, on Valencia Street, there was another drive-by. Here, three men shot, one dead. A cop on paid leave. I can't remember the last time I went outside and didn't blow up my chest and pull a hard mask over my face just to make it down the street without someone trying to start shit. And then this morning, a body was found hacked to pieces. A member of a local gang, packaged like meat, left to cook in the sun somewhere in the outskirts of Fresno.

This is not some glamorized sin city metropolis I am talking about; this is small town America. The San Joaquin Valley is a chunk of land that accounts for over 400 miles in length and 200 miles in width of California's womb, and prides itself on being the breadbasket of the world. Every town here is spread out approximately six miles from one another, because this was the distance that the Southern Pacific Railroad trains could travel before needing more water to fuel the steam engines.

Now, that last sentence is untrue. It is and it isn't. On a recent trip to visit the poet Aaron Abeyta in Antonito, Colorado, he told me that this was exactly how the towns of northern New Mexico were founded. A railroad, and a need.

Why not the San Joaquin Valley, I thought. It makes perfect sense. But here is the crazy part. Most of what is made up in this book are the small believable details. Very much like this last example. The irony is that the true stories in this book, the ones that actually happened, are the ones most unbelievable. Imagine a place of abundance, where fruit hangs from every tree on nearly every corner, and meat butchery is a practice of almost spiritual proportions. Now imagine that same place fraught with hunger and undernourishment.

As I write, the church bells across the street are ringing twelve gongs. It is midnight, and at the present moment, at least these streets are silent. Even the helicopters have given the sky a rest on this night. But around here silence is jarring. And so the dogs bark to keep from going crazy. The dogs bark, and the rest of us simply remind ourselves to breathe.

Acknowledgments

I owe a debt of gratitude to the following people: Victor Martinez, Andrew Wille, Indira Ganeson, and Jason McDonald for their valuable insight and sharp eye on some of these stories. Special thanks to my homeboys/girls, you know who you are, my deepest respect always, especially the musicos del valle—Aaron Wall, Richard Juarez, Mezcal, Ted Nunes, Jeremy Hofer, Lance Canales, and Jonas Berglund (Stockholm). Big thanks to my family: Felix Hernandez, Sr. (RIP), Estela Constante Hernandez (RIP), and to my primos y primas who know this hard landscape too well, and to Tia Hilda, my blood always. Also, to my Zuniga tribe, spiritual warriors all of you. Infinite love to my sister Delylah for having my back again and again. Across the panorama of dusty towns that make up central Califas, this one also goes out to the youth who live it, especially the old crew from Kaspian Heights, and the students at Sequoia High School, Orosi High School, Dinuba High School, La Sierra Military Academy, and Redwood High School. A deep bow to Debbie Petinak who delivered me to poetry in peach blossoms back in the third grade, and for el maestro Juan Felipe Herrera for keeping me in check. Dayanna, gracias, amor, for being my soul partner in this life and for everything you endure with me in this curious calling. Also, for brother in word and residency, Daniel Grandbois, dirty scribbler of hallucinations, and last but not least, my dear friend, editor, and hands-down the most fearless writer I know, Irene Vilar, for believing. *Namaste.*